Tales from the Forest

ʻark Billen

Black Pear Press

Tales from the Forest

Mark Billen

First published in the UK 2014 by Black Pear Press

ISBN 978-1-910322-02-4

Edited by Black Pear Press Limited

Cover photograph by Mark Billen
Cover design by Black Pear Press

Dedication

For all those people who have heard these tales and encouraged me to put them into print.

Acknowledgements

I would like to thank the editors of Black Pear Press for their support and wisdom. Without their enthusiasm I suspect that the *Tales from the Forest* would have been 'something to get published one day'. Their encouragement has made me gather up the stories into one volume.

I must also thank the people who have heard the tales; especially the members of Worcester Writers' Circle who have listened and often laughed. The response has been most rewarding and much appreciated.

Foreword

The Forest, and its villages as depicted in these tales, does not exist. Countryside stories and anecdotes, some sad, many humorous, have been gathered from far and wide. I invented a community and a range of inhabitants to give coherence.

You won't find The Forest, Whytteford, Humbury, Salchester, or any of the villages, on a map. Some people may think they recognize a village from one tale but find that another story bears no relationship to the place that they had in mind.

Contents

Whytteford

There's only the one public house in Whytteford, it's been there for well over two centuries and is called The Cobblers Arms. Every evening my great-grandfather would tell his wife that he was off to The Cobblers to get some tobacco. He'd return merry and singing some hours later with a little tobacco trailing between his fingers. Often my Great-Grandmother would stand at the gate of their cottage looking out for him.

'Have you seen George?' she'd ask passers by. 'I don't know where he can be.'

Opposite The Cobblers was a pond that was quite shallow. One night my Great-Grandfather, having drunk several pints of ale, bought his handful of tobacco and walked straight out of the door of The Cobblers and crossed the road without looking either way. He kept walking straight on over the verge and through the pond until he reached the other side whereupon he sat down.

'Come back, George! Come back!' his companions called.

'I can't walk through the pond,' Great-Grandfather George shouted back. 'I'll get my feet wet.'

The Cobblers Arms

1

Generations of my family lived in Whytteford since the end of Queen Victoria's reign. The village is thin one way but in the other direction it's long. At one end there are two church cottages that were named after a rector's children. One is Ethel Cottage and the other is Edward Cottage and they are still there with the names engraved in stone above the front doors. I often wonder if the modern inhabitants have any idea who Ethel and Edward were. My great-grandfather moved his family to the village and they lived in Edward Cottage. With it came quite an area of land where he planted apple trees and grew vegetables and potatoes.

The Forest climate is usually quite gentle so Great-Grandfather took advantage of the long growing seasons and fed his family well. In one corner of the garden there was a pigsty, as in those days it was quite normal for country people to keep a pig so that they had meat for winter meals.

In later years George used to walk with a stout stick that he had cut from the hedgerow. It was solid with a thick handle, smoothed and polished so that it shone. He used to roam the woods, fields, byways and tracks around the local villages often enjoying the company of his grandchildren, revealing to them the secrets of The Forest. He knew where badgers had their setts, where you could spy on fox cubs playing, where the kingfishers darted and where adders hid. Summer was a time for occasional longer evening walks, to visit somewhere different from The Cobblers Arms, to hear the news of other villages. After a drink or few he'd walk home in the moonlight enjoying the beauty of the forest glades where deer might be softly grazing beneath the summer night sky.

Until a few years ago there was an elderly lady living at Whytteford and she had never left the village of her birth. She could vividly remember my Great-Grandmother who always dressed in black, with a bonnet and a long white apron. Her mind wandered and she'd say strange things. To the younger children she was an old lady to avoid and of course they thought she was a witch. Great-Grandfather

George and his wife had six children who grew up and settled in nearby villages, although some later moved to more distant places.

George liked his drink and one son certainly did not approve of his father's habits and so he went to live in the north of England. He was my Great-Uncle Arthur and I met him just once. Great-Auntie Mabel was wooed by a travelling salesman and went to live in Burtonbridge. Even in old age Mabel had a twinkle in her eye. Great-Aunt Brenda lived in Brookford, which was the next village across the common, Great-Aunt Edna was not far away in the cathedral city of Salchester and my grandparents had a quaint cottage in Chamford. There was another great-uncle whose name I cannot remember as he was never mentioned!

Living in this village in The Forest was like being transported to another age. People had names such as Jonah, Ebenezer, Mildred, Silas, Ezekiah, Alberta, Zebedee, Jonah, Obidiah, Titus and Ezekiel. Even Charity and Diligence and Dimity were not unusual names. Today the older inhabitants of the village, many of whom have seldom travelled more than a few miles away, have the benefit of very distinct names that once heard are not forgotten. Although my family has associations with the village that go back over a century, none of my relations had any of these exciting monikers.

One morning my mother was waiting for the bus to Salchester and was joined by an elderly villager who asked all sorts of questions. In particular he asked about Great-Aunt Mabel.

'Tell me,' he murmured, 'is Mabel still alive?'

'Yes, she lives in Burtonbridge.'

'Not so far then.'

'We see her every few months.'

'Is she well?'

'I am sure she is.'

'Ah! Great girl, Mabel.'

'Really?'

'Wonderful,' he said in musing tone. 'By gum, that girl couldn't half run.' There was a twinkle in the elderly man's eyes. 'But she liked to be caught!' he added with a look half way between a smile and a leer. 'Happy days! Give her my love and tell her I remember Woodbine Wood!'

Once, when I was much older and feeling inquisitive, I asked Auntie Mabel about Woodbine Wood. 'Where is Woodbine Wood?' I asked innocently. 'What happens there?'

'Haven't you found it yet?' she asked with a memorable light in her eyes. 'You'll find it when you need it,' she added with a delicious touch of mystery, 'and you'll have a lovely time. Yes, a lovely time...' Great-Aunt Mabel was clearly recalling her youth. 'A lovely time...' she repeated with a now wistful look in her eyes. 'A lovely time...'

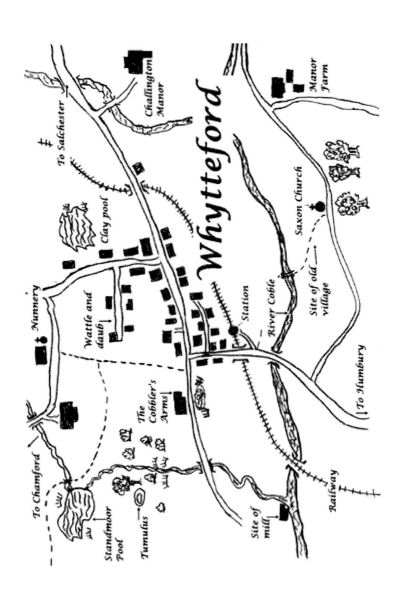

Whytteford

Chaffington Manor

Manor Farm

To Salchester

Clay pool

Saxon Church

Nunnery

Wattle and daub

Site of old village

Station

River Coble

The Cobbler's Arms

To Humbury

To Chamford

Standmoor Pool

Tumulus

Site of mill

Railway

Off To Church

Whytteford church is in a rather isolated spot in a hidden valley. Woodlands, popular with young lovers on summer evenings, are close at hand. Just along the road is Manor Farm. The current farmhouse is Tudor, with more recent additions, but the farm has been there for centuries and is listed in the Domesday Book. The Masterton family have farmed and lived there since the reign of Charles II. Traditionally the Mastertons have supported the church and usually a Masterton has been one of the churchwardens. The farm is so conveniently close to the church that when the bell starts ringing before a service the Mastertons can leave home, walk along the lane, through the lych gate, have a word with the Verger, go into church and be in the family pew before the bell stops.

When a new Rector of Whytteford arrived the then warden, Algernon Masterton, thought he should introduce him before the new incumbent took his first service. The bell had rung, the congregation had assembled and the new Rector was waiting outside the church in his robes. Algernon arrived wearing Wellington boots, rather soiled corduroy trousers, a shirt with frayed collar and cuffs and a tweed jacket with crude patches on the elbows. On his head was a checked, tweed shooting-hat, with straws sticking out of it as well as feathers from jays and magpies.

'There you are,' he said as he took control of the situation. 'Let's introduce you. You'll find they're a friendly lot.' He kicked off his Wellington boots revealing that he was wearing thick socks on his feet. Showing no concern he led the new Rector into the little Saxon church.

'Good morning, everybody,' Algernon calmly declared. 'It's lovely to see so many of you here.' There was an unusually large congregation as the villagers were keen to meet the new Rector. 'I hope you will welcome the Reverend Philip Paston to our church and enjoy the service. Now I've got to go and feed my pigs.' Having made his brief introduction the warden calmly walked out of the church, back to his farm, and the new Rector of Whytteford conducted his first service.

Reverend Paston was an imaginative man, with young children. He held services that encouraged family attendance. As well as Easter services, Harvest Festival, Carol and Christmas services that children always enjoy, he included a Spring Service when the new flowers were welcomed. Younger children brought in the flowers of a season and sat before the congregation displaying a dazzling array of blooms. In January there was a toy service when the young members of the congregation showed off favourite toys. My teddy bear must have become rather bored with these services as on one occasion, when I was no longer a small infant, he hid deep in the bedclothes and missed the event. Later he emerged with a smug look on his furry face.

When I was about six years old I began to listen to the regular Sunday services and also tried to join in the hymns, even if I was unfamiliar with them. The hymns were fairly easy to follow except when they had long words like 'immortal', 'eternal' and 'invisible' scattered through them. Psalms seemed very peculiar, making little sense to me and so I gave up trying to follow them. Bible readings, from the Authorised Version, could be very exciting or desperately dull. Some of the Old Testament readings were full of action and even a little frightening. Nobody ever explained anything about the psalms or the readings. I just accepted or was mystified by them and asked no questions.

One word in the church services I really did not understand but I gradually worked out the meaning. This word was 'forefathers'. Nobody told me what it meant. 'Four fathers,' I quietly thought. 'How can there be four fathers?'

And so I began to count.

There was God the Father. We constantly heard about him in the services so he was father number one.

There was my father, standing in the pew beside my

mother. He was father number two.

My mother's parents had died long before my parents married. I never knew them and so I did not realise that it was possible to have two grandfathers. As my father's parents were both alive I had just one grandfather. He must be father number three.

Who, then was father number four of my four fathers? I pondered this problem through many services and when I heard the word 'forefathers' I would count off the three fathers and then think about this puzzle.

Eventually the answer came to me. The mystery was solved and I was convinced that I was right. Counting on my fingers I listed the four fathers.

One was God the Father.

Two was my father.

Three was my grandfather.

And so who was father number four? The answer had come in a flash of inspiration.

Father number four was Father Christmas!

I decided that Father Christmas was one of my four fathers!

Dogged Determination

We could hear the roar of a motorbike approaching our home and the scrunch of tyres on the gravel drive. It was a powerful machine with a sidecar and peering out was a black Labrador dog.

The motorbike rider dismounted, removed his helmet and strode over to my father.

'I've heard you're looking for a dog. You can have this one. Take him or he'll be put down tomorrow.'

This was a harsh statement. My father paused for a moment before he asked, 'Why's that?'

'We can't control him. He dominates us. He snarls and growls at us if we try to get him out of a chair. He's nasty.'

'What's his name?'

'Jim.'

'We'll take him.'

The sidecar was opened and the dog climbed out. He was without a collar; there was just a rope round his neck. My father slipped his hand in his pocket then shook hands with the motorbike man. Some money had been exchanged.

'He's yours then. Good luck.' The man mounted his motorbike and drove away. We never saw that man again.

'We can't call him Jim,' said my mother. 'There's Uncle Jim and we call our scarecrow Jim. We can't have another Jim.'

'Then we'll call him Tim. That won't confuse him.'

Tim looked worried. What was he doing with these strange people? My father moved towards the house and Tim lunged forward.

'You can stop that!' He was pulled back. 'Sit!' declared my father and Tim, sensing a voice of authority, immediately obeyed.

Within three days this uncontrollable creature had become a docile, gentle and obedient dog. He was wonderful with young children, adored my mother, and was loved by all of us. He was an intelligent dog and clearly understood much more than basic commands. If we were having a busy day we had to tell him what was happening and then he would co-operate. If we didn't do this he was clearly worried and often became awkward.

Tim did not like unsettled times; he liked life to be constant and so when anything disrupted routine he would leave home for a few days. The first time that this happened we were very upset. An advertisement was placed in the Humbury Advertiser and we soon received a phone call. Tim had strayed a few miles, made friends with a family and was well cared for. On another occasion he was waiting for me outside the local school and when I had finished for the day he accompanied me home, behaving as if this was something that happened regularly.

Taking Tim for a walk was always an entertainment. If there were rabbits about, he chased them. If he found a rabbit hole, then he practised his digging. He would run off as we walked, not to be seen for several minutes, then come bounding back to find out why we were all so slow. Off he would dash exploring ahead, then returning to lead us on. But when my young cousin visited, Tim would walk patiently beside him, acting as a guide and leading the way.

Our dog was not afraid of larger animals. He would courageously run through a field of cows as if they were not there. A group of horses cropping the turf were of no concern but a stallion was treated with respect. On one occasion when I was out with him we were walking across some open common land. Tim suddenly stopped. Ahead of us were some horses. There was nothing unusual about this but when I looked ahead I saw that Streak, a tall stallion, was staring straight at us as he guarded his harem of mares. Without a word from me Tim lead the way home choosing a route behind bushes and trees that shielded us from Streak's view.

At the end of each walk Tim would pick up a stick, usually quite a large stick, and carry it home ready for the fire. After the incident with Streak I suddenly realised that this had not happened. 'Where's your stick? You haven't picked up a stick.' Tim turned back, found a thick piece of gorse and carried it home.

Tim found a thick piece of gorse and carried it home

Not all of Tim's solo excursions were because of the disturbances that made him feel unsettled. He often had amorous intent.

Not far away lived a female Labrador, a few years younger than Tim.

'I think your dog's been wandering,' announced her owner, her eyes twinkling. 'Come and have a look.'

A fine litter of Labrador puppies had been born and once they were a few weeks old several of them bore a distinct resemblance to our friend. He had indeed been wandering and even today there must be Labrador dogs in Whytteford that are descended from our dear Tim.

On one occasion he disappeared for several days and there was no news. He had a collar with name and telephone number engraved on a tag but in those days many people did not have telephones. Communication was not always easy.

Suddenly, late on a Saturday afternoon, there was a loud hammering on our back door. When the door was opened we saw an elderly man in well-worn clothes; he had a grizzled face and he carried a stout stick. He clutched a long piece of twine and on the end it was Tim.

'Hello, Mr Mander,' said my father.

'Oi gart yer dog,' snarled the man. "Ee attarked moi chickenses.'

'Oh dear, I am so sorry.'

'Oi gave'n a roight leatherin' wi' me belt.'

Tim was clearly pleased to be home and he was doing his best to edge away from Mr Mander.

"Ee killed two of 'em.'

'Have a cup of tea and some cake,' said my mother.

'Oid've brung 'im back sooner only oi couldn' fine me glarses,' he explained.

Mr Mander sat down and with tea and fruitcake inside him gradually became less aggressive. When he had finished his tea he even smiled.

'Well, better be gawn,' he said, and he stared deliberately at my father.

'Of course.' My father went out with Mr Mander and returned a few minutes later.

'How much?' my mother asked.

'Ten shillings,' said my father.

A few days later old Harry called in to see us.

'Oi hears yer dorg back'n,' he drawled.

'Yes and we're glad to have him. Unfortunately he killed two of Mr Mander's chicken.'

'Did 'e now,' mused Harry. Then he added, 'Tha's odd. Ol' Mander's nart kept chickens for o'er three years.'

Auntie Brenda's Butter

My Great-Aunt Brenda lived in a cottage in Brookford, a village on the other side of the common, and she kept a cow. When I knew her she was already very old and not very mobile. Really it was her daughter, Gertie, who looked after the cow but the animal was always referred to as Auntie Brenda's cow. I never had the honour of meeting this creature as it roamed the common but waited near the forest gate to Great-Aunt Brenda's cottage whenever milking time was approaching.

Great-Auntie Brenda kept a cow

From time to time my grandparents visited us and my grandfather thought we should go and see his oldest sister. This was an experience to be missed if at all possible, as there was always a consequence.

We would gather in a gloomy room with the ancient Brenda sitting enthroned in an even more ancient high-backed chair and holding court. I would slip into a corner near a window and immerse myself in souvenir books of Queen Victoria's Diamond Jubilee and King Edward VII's Coronation. This saved me being involved in a conversation about people I had never known, as many were long dead.

Snatches of the conversation wafted around me.

'Do you remember when Walter Gander…?'

'Then there was the time when he…'

'That was in '23 wasn't it?'

'No, Alb, it t'was '24 'cos it was the same year as…'

'You're wrong, Brenda, I know that when he…'

Really I could have joined in the conversation, as it was nearly always the same. It was as if my older relatives knew their parts in an obscure rural drama and whenever they met there had to be a rehearsal. Compared to the conversation the ancient souvenir books were fascinating.

Eventually the most dreaded part of the visit came: our departure. You would think that for me this would be the best part of the occasion but our leaving would always include a sentence of doom.

'Alb,' Brenda would say to my grandfather, 'you must have some butter.'

'No thanks, Brenda. We're all right, we've got some.'

'Don't be silly, Alb, you know you like it.'

'No…well…er…' poor Grandpa couldn't think of anything else to say.

'Gertie, get your uncle a nice pat of butter.'

Gertie would go off to the cool larder and come back with some suspiciously dark yellow butter wrapped in greaseproof paper.

'There you are, Alb, take that and enjoy it!'

These grim words ended each visit and we would take Grandma and Grandpa back to their quaint cottage at Chamford. On one occasion Grandpa had a last cunning and dreadful trick to play.

'Thank you for a good day,' he said, and then added, 'You have this butter. We've got plenty so we don't need it.' Then he thrust the pat of butter into my mother's reluctant hands.

Having endured the shortages of two wars, my mother thought that no food should be wasted and if anything was given to us it was almost a sin not to be grateful and use it.

My grandfather grew a lot of vegetables. Peas and broad beans were specialities and he never harvested them until they were full and fat. This meant that they were also as hard as bullets and almost impossible to digest but we still had to eat them.

'Grandpa grew them and gave them to us so we mustn't waste them.'

In my mind I had visions of firing bullet hard peas and beans from my backside if I should dare to break wind. What would happen if the whole family was afflicted with this problem at the same time?

But Grandpa's bullets were a delight compared with Auntie Brenda's butter. It was rancid, it was disgusting and it was vile but because it was a gift we were expected to eat it.

'What am I to say if we throw it away?' asked my mother who was a truly honest person.

Eventually my father put his foot down. 'It's not fit to eat.'

'But what shall we do with it? We can't waste it.'

'Then Tim will have to eat it.'

Tim was our delightful black Labrador dog. He ate everything at any time and was normally an obliging doggy dustbin. You couldn't have a more willing, obedient and affectionate dog than Tim.

You couldn't have a more willing, obedient and
affectionate dog than Tim

15

Some of the butter was spread on Tim's dog biscuits and we called him in.

The plate with the biscuits butter side down was put before him. Normally they might have lasted a couple of minutes.

This time dear Tim took one deep sniff, wrinkled his nose, turned round and went outside.

'Oh dear,' said my mother. 'I'll have to make a cake with the rest of it.'

'You'll do no such thing,' my father replied.

'What ever shall we tell Auntie Brenda?'

'We don't need to tell her anything. It won't be a problem...just remember,' my father said with a knowing wink, 'the butter wasn't given to us!'

Grandma's Medicine

I can remember that autumn day vividly. I had just walked home from school on a path through The Forest. When I reached the house my parents weren't there but my brother had returned before me and read a message that had been left for us.

'Mum and Dad have had to go to Chamford. Grandma's very ill.' It never crossed my mind that 'very ill' meant that my wonderful grandmother was likely to die. She was one of the kindest, most patient and loving people that I have ever known. She knitted me jumpers. She crocheted delicate mats. When teddy bears needed clothes she knitted them outfits that fitted perfectly. She even made them hats, scarves and gloves for their paws so that the bears would keep warm in winter. For these special items there were no patterns, Grandma just knew what to do and the garments almost seemed to knit themselves as she seldom looked to see what she was doing.

Eventually my parents came home for the evening. I think the shock of the news must have had an effect on my brother and me as for once we had been very amicable whilst we were left alone. A doctor had come to see our grandmother and explained that she had suffered a severe stroke. How long would she live?

'Who knows?' he replied. 'Five minutes, five hours, five weeks, five months or even five years? Who knows?'

I had no idea what a stroke was and in those days such things were not explained to children.

Each evening my parents travelled to Chamford to see if Grandma was recovering and how my grandfather was coping. They usually returned after my bedtime and so I didn't really know what was going on.

After a few days I asked, 'Can I come and see Grandma?'

'I don't see why not,' said my father. 'It might do her good.'

When we reached my grandparents' cottage I went in to

the bedroom. Grandma was propped up in bed. 'Hello,' she whispered and she tried to manage a smile. I looked at her. What had happened to my grandma? She could barely speak, she lay motionless and her head was twisted out of shape. It was then that I realised the seriousness of the situation.

Five days passed and so did five weeks and even five months. Grandma was still very much alive. Her head gradually untwisted, her eyes twinkled and she could speak very clearly. Sadly she lost the use of her left arm and left leg and so she had to be in a wheelchair. Her cheeky sense of humour returned. 'I'm here for a while yet,' she said, 'after all a cracked pitcher lasts longest.' She was right: five years passed and Grandma, restricted though she was, was still with us and enjoying her curious life.

Grandma was prescribed a variety of medicines or tonics all of which were declared disgusting. Little glasses of carefully measured medicaments were put beside her ready to be swallowed. 'I'll have that later, I don't want the taste of it to spoil my lunch,' Grandma would say and she was so stubborn that there was no point in arguing. Sometime later the medicine glass was empty.

There was always a houseplant here and there in Grandma and Grandpa's cottage and so that they received enough light they were near the windows, just where Grandma sat in her chair reading her magazines. I realised that the foliage of one of these plants was gradually changing colour. What was going on? The answer was simple, as this particular plant was receiving a daily dose of Grandma's medicine. 'It's good for the plants,' she privately told me, 'better for them than for me.' I kept her secret and wondered what else might happen. The plants occasionally moved around and a different one would be next to Grandma. One perfectly healthy bowl of daffodils wilted and died in five days. 'I'd better not do that again,' Grandma muttered quietly, and from then on she would also swash her medicine into the air and it would disappear into the heavily patterned carpet.

Another plant, a 'Busy Lizzie', grew at a phenomenal rate producing an abundance of unusually deep red flowers. The more medicine it received the better it grew. The flowers were glorious and particularly large.

'That's a fine plant,' the doctor declared when he visited. 'What are you feeding it?'

'Nothing special,' said Grandma. 'Something I can get quite easily.'

This particular plant was receiving a daily dose of Grandma's medicine

Grandma's secret was safe with me as I was intrigued to see what else might happen. Would superfast and super strength plant growth result in Grandma becoming engulfed by a giant aspidistra?

On summer days she would sit in the garden by her little pond that held a few goldfish that spent most of their time hiding under the lily leaves. If nobody was with her, the fish were treated to a dose of Grandma's disgusting medicine. Naturally it became highly diluted and so the dose was very mild. What might happen if the fish received a constant dose of medicine? One summer the rains stopped and the sunshine spread through The Forest and into the little cottage garden. Every day Grandma sat by the pond and the fish received their medicine. Nothing happened that was noticeable until one day when I was sitting nearby and I heard a SPLOSH. Grandma had thrown her medicine into the pond again! I looked below the surface. A large goldfish was eagerly gulping the slightly reddish brown water where the mixture had splashed. 'Gulp, gulp, and gulp!' The fish was enjoying the medicine. A few gulps and it swam away. What would happen? Would there soon be deep maroon goldfish in the pond? Would they become as big as pike? Would they change personality and become aggressive? The summer passed and nothing dramatic happened but the fish carried on enjoying their daily treat. I suppose they must have missed their medicine when the autumn came.

Five minutes, five hours, five weeks, five months or even five years? How long would Grandma live after her stroke? In fact she lived for over thirteen years. As she said, 'Cracked pitchers last longest.'

Marrow Rum

The problem began before I was born. My parents were given a marrow, not any ordinary marrow but a very large marrow. This was a most unwelcome gift as my father wouldn't contemplate eating it and my mother had no idea what else to do. It sat neglected for a few days until someone made a suggestion. 'You could always make marrow rum. I'll give you the recipe.'

That is why the marrow rum was made. This involved much boiling and numerous packets of sugar being added to the pan. Eventually the rum had been ready apart from one ingredient that needed to be added once the liquid had cooled. The missing constituent was a bottle of rum. The reason it was never added was that at the time my parents simply could not afford to buy the rum. Out of respect for the amount of sugar that had been used the light amber liquid was poured into bottles of varying sizes and shapes, corks were rammed home and the six bottles were put into a crate and forgotten.

At some point in this history I was born. Every few years there would be a grand clear out of accumulated defunct machines, old bikes and gardening tools and the marrow rum would emerge.

'What's that?' I asked.

'Marrow rum.'

'Can you drink it?'

'It needs more time.'

This answer baffled me. The crate was put away in a dark and gloomy place awaiting the next clear out.

My mother began to make a Christmas cake and discovered some raisins that had been kept too long; they were disguised by a light grey sheen. She was about to throw them away.

'Don't throw them out, we'll put them in the marrow rum.'

I should point out that by now these mysterious bottles

had been with my family for over ten years and the most exciting thing that had ever been done to the marrow rum in a decade was about to occur. The bottles were taken from their dark place, stoppers were removed and the exciting additive of mildewed raisins was inserted.

Sometime later my brother was given a ginger beer plant. Once a day he fed it with ginger and sugar and each week, when he made ginger beer, half of the plant had to be thrown away. The inevitable happened.

'Don't throw that away, we'll put some in the marrow rum.'

The marrow rum emerged from the gloom, the bottles were opened again and some ginger beer plant was added to the golden liquid and the darkening raisins. The concoction was then duly hidden away at the back of the garage. It survived a bitter winter without the bottles cracking open in the cold; perhaps the contents now had some of the qualities of antifreeze.

One spring my father decided to buy a new vehicle and it was to be kept in the garage. This caused a major upheaval during which the wooden crate was rediscovered. By now woodworm had attacked and it more or less collapsed when moved. The bottles were intact, each with some curious light brown and lumpy sediment. The so-called rum was now a rich amber colour.

'Gosh, the marrow rum!'

'It must be vintage marrow rum by now.'

'Wonderful colour.'

'Let's try some.'

The almost syrupy liquid was decanted, small glasses filled and the official tasting began. It was potent and had a unique flavour; rich, sweet, slightly gingery and without any hint of marrow. We decided to decant this rare liquor from the other bottles.

When we reached the final bottle the cork was missing. The explanation was there before us. A mouse had nibbled through the cork, slid through the neck of the bottle and drowned itself in the amber fluid. It was complete, totally pickled, with its tail vertical and neatly pointing up the neck of the bottle; an unusual death for a mouse.

Naturally, this additional content meant that the decanting from the final bottle had to proceed with extra care.

An unusual death for a mouse

Truth Between Sneezes

Old Harry had always lived in Whytteford. He had never thought of moving away and was totally content with a simple and unhurried life. He had attended the village school with my grandfather.

'Ah,' he'd say. 'Your grandfar was the best-behaved boy in the class and I was the wors'n. Ah!' He spoke with the rich forest accent using dialect words many of which have now faded away. Occasionally Grandfather and Harry met and began chatting. The longer they chatted the stronger the dialect grew until I struggled to understand a sentence.

'Bis'n you doing that?'

'Ney, nos'n more. Makes me come over all leer, an then I bis'n 'n cas'n as summit stops the zoiv being zarp.'

'Yer waach yersel, Alb. Nah, lit's ave kiddle o taay.'

'Not towday.'

'Yoo'll bee yeer too-morrur, woant dhee?'

And so it went on. Fortunately when I chatted to Harry he spoke in a more normal way, admittedly through a thick moustache, but with care he could be understood. On one occasion my homework for the weekend was to interview someone who was old and write down a story from the past. Old Harry was the obvious choice as he had lived in the same village all his life. It was seven o'clock on an early autumn evening but that was too late for seeing Harry. He went to bed about eight o'clock as it kept him warm and it was cheaper than lighting a fire.

'Go and see him about ten o'clock in the morning,' said my father, 'Harry's at his best then.'

When I found him he was in the garden of his cottage dealing with some emmets.

'Good morning, Harry,' I said. Now this may seem disrespectful but everyone just called him Harry.

'Helloo, youg'n, ow be-ist?' This much I could translate.

'What are you doing?' I asked.

'Weall, therez emmets jus'ere, and I bisn'n 'aving ney

emmets.'

'Emmets?' I asked.

'Ay emmets, I gaw some pawder to kiell the emmets thar.'

He held up a container of ant powder and I understood what he meant.

'Av I evar told youm abart the emmets at the varm?'

'No,' I said, sensing a story that would be good for my work.

'Well, tis like this'n.' Suddenly Harry gave a huge sneeze. 'Thar,' he said, 'Oi've snazed so now you'm knaws what I saez is true!'

Old Ezekiah Turridge didn't take much care of his farm. He had a little herd of four milking cows and every day he took them into the milking shed. The trouble was a great pile of earth had built up by the milking shed. Dropped from horses hooves and cart wheels the earth was just shovelled up by the wall of the milking shed, right under a window. After a while ants built a nest in the pile of soil and from there it was easy for them to get into the milking shed. They climbed through a crack in the wall and the soil from the nest spread. It spread through the wall cracks and the ants' nest spread as well. Soon ants had taken up residence in the milking shed. Twice every day Ezekiah brought his cows in for milking; he milked them by hand and the fresh warm milk squirted from the cows' udders straight into the buckets. He would put it in his little dairy to cool so that the cream could be separated. Everyone close by bought milk from Ezekiah as it was good milk and as fresh as you could buy.

'In the caow one day 'nd on table nex' day,' explained Harry.

'Wasn't it pasteurised?' I asked.

'We niver bathered with things loik that, didn' need too.'

The inevitable happened. A few ants' eggs fell in the milk one day and being as white as the milk they weren't noticed.

The milk was sold and nothing happened but a few days later Maudie Grannage said she was feeling funny in her stomach. It went on for days and days until eventually she went to see Doctor Rundell. He examined Maudie but couldn't find a thing wrong with her, yet she kept on having funny feelings. What's more they were getting worse and some nights poor Maudie couldn't sleep.

A great pile of earth had built up by the milking shed

One day Maudie suddenly had a coughing fit and emmets began streaming out of her mouth.

'Help me! Help me!' she cried and folks tried slapping her on the back to make the emmets all come up. Suddenly she gave another big cough and the horrible procession stopped.

A week or so after she felt the same funny feelings. 'I don't want emmets again,' said Maudie. She went to see the doctor a second time but he was at a loss. He listened to her with his stethoscope yet even with that there was nothing to be heard. His only advice was to drink plenty of hot tea. Then he said not to eat anything for three days hoping to starve the emmets but it made no difference. Maudie had another coughing fit and the same thing happened only worse. The emmets came streaming out of her mouth, more and more and more. Poor Maudie was writhing and twisting.

Someone said she should drink boiling water but of course she couldn't. Then old Mrs Dawkings said she knew what to do. Emmets hate anything to do with soap. Mrs Dawkings told Maudie to drink soapy water, lots of it and the soapier the better. Poor Maudie could hardly get it down it tasted so vile but she tried and tried, as she wanted to be cured. She began to cough and cough and then her mouth had foam bubbling out of it. The more she coughed the more the bubbles came. She gave a mighty heaving cough and up came a ball of ants' eggs and some nasty smells and a lot more bubbles. After that Maudie didn't feel quite right for a few days but her insides were as clean as could be. She drank four bottles of dandelion wine to get rid of the taste of the soap.

Suddenly old Harry gave another big sneeze.

'Thar,' he said, 'anything said between snazes is alwuss true!'

'Really?'

'Carse it yis!'

I saw my grandfather a few days later. 'Do you remember Maudie Grannage?' I asked.

'Maudie Grannage?' he said. 'No…I don't remember her. No-one of that name ever lived round here.'

The Drunken Rector

Great-Aunt Edna had tales to tell of life in Whytteford including events in the ancient church. This tiny building is curiously at one side of the village, away from the area of cottages and The Cobblers Arms. Built in Saxon times the structure has barely altered in over one thousand years. It has been re-roofed and a balcony was added in the Victorian era but otherwise it has been left untouched. Saxon wall paintings have even survived, possible because the little church is so tucked away that Cromwell's men decided not to bother with it. Until quite recently the church did not have an organ; it had a harmonium that had seen better days when Edna was young and it was still in use when she died aged 87.

Edna used to delight in telling the tale of one member of the congregation, Zebedee Gramble, who always sat on the front row in the church balcony. When the rector began to preach his sermon he'd put his feet up and fall asleep. The reason for this was that the rector, Rev. Albion Augustus Mountjoy, would give long sermons of considerable erudition that were beyond the comprehension of most of the congregation and they certainly didn't suit Zebedee. Often he would fall deeply asleep and begin to snore. The younger members of the congregation found his snores of greater interest than the rector's sermon. The big question would always be how many snores would the portly Zebedee give before they became so loud that he woke himself up?

On one occasion a bluebottle was buzzing around the church balcony and Zebedee was soundly asleep. He had a red and bulbous nose that provided a generous landing ground for a fly. Everyone in the church balcony watched intently waiting for the fly to rest on Zebedeee. After a few diversions it settled on the ample space that his nose provided but Zebedee just slept on. The younger members of the congregation began to giggle, which rather surprised the rector, as he never put anything remotely humorous into his sermons. The bluebottle, having found a comfortable place, made no attempt to fly away, it just explored Zebedee's rosy nose. Wasn't it tickling him? Apparently not, as he continued to sleep through the sermon, that by this time was receiving little attention. Everyone who was watching held their breath and then gasped as the fly moved to the very tip of Zebedee's nose, took off, then buzzed around before settling in exactly the same spot. This triggered something as Zebedee gave a mighty sneeze, looked about the church, and settled back to sleep as the Rev. Mountjoy continued his sermon.

The rector lived in a mansion some way from the church. When Rev. Mountjoy was in office you always visited him in the early part of the day as from lunchtime onwards he began drinking. Somehow on the Sabbath he managed to control himself until after evensong then he must have made up for lost time, as he was apparently never available on Mondays.

The benefice was taken away from the drunken Rector

News of his little problem reached the Bishop of Salchester and the benefice was taken from the drunken rector. One night, before he left the parish, he decided in his inebriated state that he must clear up all the paperwork. Although it was midsummer he lit a fire in the great fireplace of the mansion, made sure it was burning well and gradually cleared up all the paperwork connected with Whytteford Church and the church school. The fire blazed and the villagers wondered what on earth was happening as well into the night the windows glowed with the light of flickering flames. The next morning Rev. Albion Augustus Mountjoy left the rectory behind him; and a string of problems that affected the church and village school for decades.

Sphagnum Moss

The Forest has many a marshy place and if a walker is not aware of what to look for these soft spots can be traps for the unwary. The sphagnum moss soaks up the water of pools, streams and boggy places to an astonishing extent, absorbing many times its own weight. The surface of the sphagnum moss can be dangerously inviting, especially in very dry weather. The top dries off and the moss looks like part of the general landscape.

School had finished for the summer. There had been several weeks without rain and the common land, including the marshy mossy areas, had dried out. Paths that could sometimes have wet and hazardous sections were dry and safe. The sun was shining brightly, the sky was blue, the evening was warm and after weeks of study I was wonderfully free, as no homework had to be completed. What a wonderful evening to explore the delights of Whytteford Common and parts of The Forest beyond.

I set out without special footwear; it wasn't needed as everywhere was dry. I walked down to a stream and using a few stones, conveniently placed across it, strode across the clear water that lightly trickled down to join the River Coble. I climbed the gentle slope up to Parrot's Leap; a hill with a curious name; then on in to The Forest. I traversed common land, walked over smooth turf cropped short by rabbits, crossed lanes and strolled through woods. Was I lost? Of course I was lost but not far away was Stagstone Hill and if I climbed to the top I would see my way home.

On I went until the hill was in front of me and close by was a smooth mossy spot surrounded by fresh green birch trees. This looked so tempting and so delightful I had to explore. Soon I was walking on what looked to be greenish pale turf with an unusual texture. Suddenly the turf moved as I walked across it. I wasn't walking on turf; I was walking over a smooth area of sphagnum moss that gently responded to my movements. How intriguing! The land was moving as I walked.

What if I jumped?

Jump!

Up into the air I went and down on to the moss. As I landed the thick layer of moss flexed around me. It was as if I had caused a very minor earth tremor. This was new and fascinating. What if I jumped higher?

Jump!

I landed and the moss flexed and shook beneath my weight! I jumped again before the moss wave had subsided. I didn't sense any danger; my feet didn't sink into the moss as the top layer was so pale and dry. My experiment over I climbed Stagstone Hill; planned my route and calmly walked home.

The Forest's wet and boggy places became
more treacherous than ever

Little did I realise the danger I had narrowly avoided. The hot summer sun had baked the sphagnum moss where I had walked. The top of it had been dried so that it held no water. Because of its crisped state I had escaped the death trap that sphagnum moss can so easily be. The moss layer was thick, but down below the moss was wet as ever; only the top was dry. I had been walking and jumping in places that at other times hid dangers. The following autumn I tried to find the route to cross the stream and as I walked on the now soaking moss my boots sunk in and I hastily retreated.

As each December approached gatherers came to collect moss for Christmas wreathes. They would carry huge wicker baskets to the marsh and pick sphagnum moss, squeeze out all the water and fill their baskets. Using boards they would walk further over the marsh gathering moss until baskets were full. They were careful and knew well the dangers that were close at foot. A false step and a man could be deep in the marsh; any movement was useless as struggling made the victim sink further in to the moss's greedy suction. One day a young gatherer, momentarily distracted, stepped from the boards and in a couple of seconds was deep into the moss's cold, wet grasp. Boards were pushed across the moss and his father lay upon them to reach his son. More boards were slid over the dangerous ground and another man was soon reaching out to the moss's victim. Together the men pulled and gradually the youth was rescued from the cruel grasp of one of The Forest's hidden dangers. He was safe but the marsh had seized his rubber boots. A mustard bath at The Cobblers Arms and a hot drink with some suitable strengthening restored the young man's temperature but he never went moss gathering again.

Wet weather continued and the dangers of The Forest's wet and boggy places became even more treacherous. The animals of The Forest usually knew where danger lay and could avoid it. Instinct and natural inbred caution normally kept them safe, but sometimes even the animals were caught unaware.

Donkeys have a curious harsh cry that travels across the air for a great distance. They roam the common lands patiently plodding on their way. Donkeys are not fussy eaters. They munch at young growth on bushes, even spiky gorse bushes, as well as cropping the turf.

Perhaps it was the temptation of a tasty leaf or two on a willow bush that made one donkey take some steps too far. Late on a gloomy autumn afternoon we heard a donkey's agonised call as it struggled against the sphagnum moss's clenching suction. Louder and louder came the call. The animal struggled and the marsh's power gradually overwhelmed the agonised creature. Night fell and the sound of the donkey's distressed braying sounded louder and carried further in the cold air. As it weakened the calls became less frequent and eventually ended. The sphagnum moss of the marsh had claimed another victim.

The Hedgehopper And The Bedstead

'Hedgehopper' - A pilot who flies his aeroplane very close to the ground, especially an aeroplane used in spraying pesticides and insecticides on crops or to attack enemies in a war.

The Forest was largely unaffected by World War Two. Most of the inhabitants were either too old to be called up or worked in reserved occupations. My grandfather, who worked on the railway, nevertheless told some curious tales of the war. You would expect him to tell of narrow escapes with trains or the bombing of docks and industrial areas, instead he told tales of war in The Forest.

As well as his railway work my grandfather found time to do some mowing at Challington Manor. Here there was a grass tennis court and Grandpa would prepare it for weekend house parties. During the war important people were welcomed by Lord and Lady Dusbury and they were given a relaxing weekend that contrasted with the intensity of their war work. On a Friday Grandfather would check the ground in case any moles had dared to ruin the lawn. If they had, the molehills would be flattened and rolled, a square of turf replaced, and then the mowing would begin. Grandpa was a very patient man with a mower. Despite the size of a tennis court he always used a hand mower. This was virtually essential during the war to save precious fuel for more important things.

Late one Friday afternoon Grandpa had finished his mowing and begun to put down the white lines. Suddenly he heard the sound of an aeroplane. He looked about and above but could see nothing and as it was a sunny summer's day he took no notice and carried on marking the lines. The noise of the plane grew closer and louder but still there was no sign of it so the work carried on. Then there was a roaring sound and the plane bobbed up over a hedge with its propeller working hard.

Grandpa stared in astonishment as all of a sudden he was

sharing the tennis court with a small and light German aeroplane that didn't quite land but flew at hedge level, a few feet from the ground. The pilot was at the controls and behind him sat a machine gunner, who momentarily stared at Grandpa and then swung the gun round. As he did so Grandpa threw himself on the ground behind the lining machine, which offered very little protection. There was a crisp rattle of bullets from the machine gun and a loud ping. The aeroplane's engine picked up speed, roared a little and it lifted up in to the air.

Grandfather picked himself up and was surprised to find that he was undamaged. The lining machine had a slight dent but was otherwise uninjured. Looking over the tennis lawn Grandfather saw a few chunks of turf scattered about and a few bullets lodged in the soil. More amused than frightened he carried on with his work. A moment later the figure of Lady Dusbury came running across the lawn.

'What has happened?'

'Just an 'edgehopper,' Grandpa replied.

'But you could have been shot.'

'But I wasn't; 'e couldn't keep still long enough to shoot me!'

'Now, you must come and have a cup of tea to calm you down,' said the flustered Lady Dusbury.

She could be very persuasive and Grandfather didn't want to seem rude. Her ladyship sat him on the terrace and made tea for them both. He began to drink the tea but after a few sips thought it tasted rather strange. Good manners prevented him making any comment.

'I hope that's doing you good,' said Lady Dusbury. 'I put a shot of whisky in to calm your nerves.' And she then drank a cup in almost indecent haste. 'It's certainly calmed my nerves, anyway.'

Grandpa, who was teetotal, admitted that he finished the white lines in record time that afternoon and slept very well that night. When he saw the lines a few days later he realized that they weren't quite as straight as usual.

Whytteford, being not far from the coast and a major port, the distant drone of German bombers was often heard at night but that was the closest that the attackers usually came as any attempt at bombing The Forest's trees, heath land, farms and scattered villages would have been futile. One clear night a German aeroplane must have suffered from failed navigation aids as the menacing drone of its engine awakened almost everyone. The droning came closer and closer dominating the still night air. People looked from their windows and could make out the crisp shape of the plane. Suddenly there was the sound of 'Crumph! Crumph! Crumph!' and the drone then faded as the German plane flew on. Those who stayed awake and listened heard a couple more distant explosions, but nothing else occurred. There was no sign of distress and nobody heard a call for help.

Ebenezer Burdon lived in a wattle and daub cottage close by Manor Farm, which had been in the direct path of the errant German bomber. Ebby was a deep sleeper and he must have been the only person in Whytteford not woken by the drone. The plane droned closer and closer but Ebby slept on. Perhaps the crew saw the cluster of farm buildings below and having a few bombs left decided that they might as well be dropped instead of returning them to Germany. They missed the farm completely but one of the bombs scored a direct hit on Ebby's cottage. 'Crumph!' went the bomb as it crashed through the thatch. It hit the floor with a 'woomph' and a blast that swept upwards into the remainder of the cottage, powering up under Ebby's bedstead! It lifted the bed and carried it up through the gap where a moment before the thatch had been in place. Ebby's garden had a few trees close by the cottage and gravity landed his bedstead in one of the trees where it held fast. The cottage had been largely destroyed but Ebenezer Burdon and his bed had survived the bombing of Whytteford.

Next morning work began as normal at the farm but where

was Ebby? The farmhands went to his cottage and were shocked by the remains that they saw, but of Ebby there was no sign.

'Ebby! Ebby!' they called and eventually they heard a sound.

'Ain't that summat like snoring?'

Ebenezer Burdon and his bed had survived the bombing of Whytteford

They looked up and saw Ebby up in the apple tree in his bed and sound asleep. The farm hands fetched a long ladder and rescued him.

"Ow come you were asleep up there, Ebby?'

'Well,' he said, 'I knew I was safe so what else was there to do?'

'You'm be darned lucky, Ebby.'

'I know I am,' said Ebby, 'but I tell you this, I couldn't 'alf eat some breakfast!'

38

The Tumulus

Much of Whytteford is adjacent to a common that is wild and open. It is an intriguing place to explore. We had a gateway leading directly to the common and so it was only natural that I often went out on my own or with friends to see what we could find.

Heather and gorse bushes abounded with the odd sprinkling of stunted silver birches. Following pony and rabbit tracks, we went wherever they took us. As long as we kept some tall pine trees in view behind us we could soon find a way back. We saw the ponies and the cows that the local commoners turned out. Often we would see riders on their horses and ponies enjoying the open spaces and giving their mounts and themselves a rare degree of freedom.

On the far side of the common was oak woodland. If we went there in the autumn we saw the pigs that were put out to eat the thousands of acorns. These are dangerous for horses to consume but seem to be a porcine delicacy.

Adventuring and enjoying the wilds of the common, I one day discovered a circle of earth with a sheltered hollow in the middle. It was virtually surrounded by gorse bushes and a few stunted birch trees. Rabbit holes were evident and there were telltale signs of occupation. Ponies and rabbits kept the turf cropped short. Here was a little hideaway. Peering between the bushes one could see yet not be seen. It was such a thrilling place for a boy to find.

Studying a local map one day I saw the word 'Tumulus' marked in several places on the common. This was a new word to me but it sounded like something ancient, as indeed it was. The tumulus I had found was unspectacular and almost completely hidden. Once I discovered that it was a prehistoric burial mound I had hopes of making some exciting archaeological discovery. Perhaps I expected the rabbits to do the work for me as whenever I visited the tumulus I always failed to take a trowel to do some excavation. I never found silver, bronze, gold or copper artefacts but as I grew older I realized that this secluded spot had special uses.

Taking my much younger cousin for a walk across the common I thought he might find the tumulus interesting. As we approached we saw two horses tethered to a nearby stunted tree and, having learnt discretion, I decided that this was not a time to visit the tumulus, especially as I knew that one horse belonged to a shapely young lady with whom I'd had dalliance before and would do so again. She liked a good ride.

'There's people there. We'll see it another time,' I said.

'I expect they're having a picnic,' my eight-year-old cousin responded.

When hormones and testosterone were rampant a delightful girl came to Whytteford to stay with her aunt. It was decided that we should meet.

'Come and have tea and then you'll meet Amanda. She needs some young company.'

And so I went to tea. I soon learnt that Amanda preferred to be called Mandy and somehow that name suited her much better. Her chestnut hair gleamed, she sparkled, her eyes beamed and her smile melted. In a very short time I was enchanted. She was wearing clinging trousers and her blouse had several buttons undone revealing tantalizing glimpses.

Chatting to her was easy and delightful; we both felt relaxed in each other's company. We talked about books, music, our hopes and plans, and the time flew by.

'How long are you here for?'

'Three weeks, and I'll be here again soon.'

'I hope we can meet again.'

'You can show me some of The Forest,' she half whispered and flashed a smile.

The tumulus was soon visited and then visited again and again. That summer there were many beautiful days but some were memorable for special reasons. Evenings were warm and our walks to the tumulus were regular. Mandy often wore tight shorts and a thin blouse that revealed most of her tempting breasts. Following this lovely girl along a narrow path would have been enough to set any young man's pulse racing.

Kissing and caressing each other in the warm evening air was my teenage idea of heaven. Then we'd talk happily before romance and lust took over once more. On one hot night we suddenly heard the sound of approaching hooves. The gorse had closed in and there was no view in the right direction.

'I'd better check.'

'Don't be long.'

I disappeared through some bushes. The sounds had come from a few roaming forest ponies that were now cropping the turf. In the clear evening air the view was spectacular.

'Nothing to worry about,' I called out.

'Come back!'

I returned to the hidden tumulus to find an even better view awaiting me. The summer sun had bronzed her body and Mandy had worked very hard to achieve an all over tan. She lay with a welcoming smile, the evening was warm, the swallows were sweeping through the air but we were hidden from the rest of The Forest. Who could resist? I fell into her willing arms and eagerly enjoyed exploring every inch of her nubile, bronzed body. The sun had set before our passion subsided and we walked away from the tumulus as the stars began to shine.

The Swallows were sweeping through the air

41

That was a very good summer: we walked, we talked, we kissed, we cuddled, we loved. Sometimes we ventured further across the common to the woodlands where the woodbine grew, and as Great-Aunt Mabel had promised, we did indeed have a lovely time in Woodbine Wood.

Master Of The Hunt

Living in The Forest we inevitably saw the hunt from time to time. Foxes abounded but usually they somehow seemed to escape the attention of the hunt. Often they were wilier than the hounds and had a cunning trick or two that must have saved many a fox. I saw one fox bound through a field full of cows. Country pancakes were in abundance and the fox was not fussy about where it trod. That certainly put the hounds off their scent!

A railway line ran through Whytteford and parts of it were hidden in a cutting with fields on either side. Jim Sawyer was a train driver and the hunt could often be seen from the train. One afternoon Jim saw the hunt coming towards the railway pursuing a fox that was well in the lead. When it reached the top of the cutting the fox paused, looked back at his pursuers and waited as the train approached. At the last moment it raced down the side of cutting, in front of Jim's train, then up the other side. The hounds and horses were cut off as the train went through and the fox escaped.

The fox escaped

As a family we were neither in favour of the hunt nor opposed to it provided it kept away from our land and did not damage the crops. This was not always the case. On one occasion hounds tore through the hedgerow following a fox. Father was furious, as he knew horses and huntsmen would soon follow. He stormed out to the common adjacent to his property and stood fuming as several horses approached with red-faced huntsmen in matching red coats.

'Where is he? Where is he?' demanded a huntsman.

Choosing his words deliberately my father responded, 'Your *dogs* are on my land! Get them off! Now!'

'Where's the fox?'

'Get your *dogs* away. I have written to the Master forbidding entry to my land! Get those dogs off!'

'Hounds, sir, we call them hounds!'

There was much shrill whistling and then horses and hounds retreated. Another irate letter was sent to the Master of the Hunt who arrived a few days later in his half-timbered car. He had a whiff about him that combined horse, hound, fox, saddle soap and leather. His face was rubicund and his red hair drifted out from beneath his tweedy cap. His boots were glowing, his breeches freshly laundered.

'I see your problem,' he declared. 'In future we'll station a boy with a whip to keep the hounds away. If there's any more problems let me know.'

This earned him considerable respect and he was true to his word. A few weeks later the hunt was about again and a figure could be seen near the hedge. To show his appreciation my father went to greet and thank him. A well-weathered, red faced, gnarled, white-haired man with legs that suggested a life with horses, stood there holding a long whip.

'Thank you for coming.'

'S'alright. S'what Master said me to do.'

'No boy available today?'

'I am the boy,' he growled. He produced a hip flask, took

a huge swig then snapped the lid shut. 'Seventy percent proof.'

'The whisky?'

'No! Me blood! Keeps me dry on the inside.'

He did a good job and we had no further trouble from the hounds.

The consequence of contact with the hunt was that our address somehow strayed on to their mailing lists. We received invitations to hunt balls, horsy events of all descriptions and even the hunting season annual report, which revealed useful information about how many braces of fox were killed by the hunt. The average was less than a brace per outing. If the foxes could have read the report they would have had a good laugh.

We enjoyed the most cordial relations with the Master of the Hunt. He was always happy to have a chat about rural matters and he had the sense to respond to any contact within a few days and to make sure problems were sorted out. He never expected a gate to be opened as gates were for jumping. On one occasion he jumped a hedge that hid a small car parked close under it. His magnificent hunter clipped the car with its hooves. The hunter was not damaged but the car bore several wounds to its paintwork. Terribly embarrassed, the Master sent his wife to the horrified owners of the car to offer apologies!

To say the Master he died in the saddle would be an exaggeration but he was certainly riding a few days before his sudden death. The Master's funeral was held at Whytteford's tiny historic church. Every pew was well filled and even the balcony seats were occupied, something the rector could not recollect previously happening during his tenure. All of the chosen hymns were traditional ones that the hunting set knew well. The singing was very hearty and lusty as the hunting fraternity didn't seem to moderate their voices when they were not hunting in the open air.

After the service the Master's coffin was taken in procession to the freshly dug grave. Standing beside it was a man immaculately dressed in the glorious scarlet known as hunting pink. In his hand he held a polished hunting horn. The bearers slowly lowered the Master's coffin into the grave and the rector presided as earth was scattered and clattered on to the lid. Suddenly the huntsman gave a shrill blast on the hunting horn, lowered it and, giving every word its maximum value, pronounced in stentorian tones that must have disturbed the sleep of the inhabitants of the graveyard: 'Gone to earth!'

Jeb Carpenter

Jeb Carpenter was a man of many talents. He could be a thatcher, a plucker of pheasants, turkeys and geese, or a wattle maker. He could help with the harvest or the ploughing whenever he was needed. He kept chicken so he had income from the eggs that he sold. He grew an abundance of vegetables and his apple trees were laden with fine fruit every September, ready to be sold from a little stall outside his cottage. Apples that were 'fallers' were pressed to make cider and that went on sale too. If you needed a tree felled, you asked Jeb to do it and he'd clear up as well, selling logs to homes with open fires. With this mixture of talents Jeb had a very good income that was far more than any farm worker. If times were slack for a while, Jeb didn't mind as he always had some money put by and there was plenty to do as he could 'turn his hand' to so many things.

Jeb knew the history of the village. Many thought that the name Whytteford originally referred to the water at the village ford running over white stones but that was not true; the stones were grey. Jeb knew that William the Conqueror had given a manor, close by the ford, to Godfrey de Whytte and so it was once known as Whytte's ford. As the decades passed this was shortened to the present name even though the Whytte family ceased to exist long ago.

Jeb knew why the church was so far from the rest of the village and why the Saxon wall paintings had partially survived. The church is so tucked away that even today it is easily missed. Oliver Cromwell's men never found the church and in a very Royalist area nobody would have shown them where it was.

Springtime visitors were told that the cuckoo came to Whytteford on April 13th each year, and unless the weather was unusually harsh that's when it arrived. On April 12th Whytteford people would say, 'We'll hear the cuckoo tomorrow,' and they were usually right.

In Jeb's grandfather's time what we called 'the main road'

had been little more than a wide gravel track that wended through The Forest to Salchester. Really it was part of an old pack way used by merchants in Medieval times as they went to and from Boshampton with valuable loads on heavily laden horses. Drovers had also used the route to drive stock to Salchester market. The road remained unsurfaced until the 1930's, when a clanking steamroller was used to create a hard surface. Jeb would show an old photograph of the roller outside The Cobblers Arms.

In one spot there was a length of wide green turf bounded by hedges. The animals that roamed The Forest kept it cropped. 'That's the old racecourse,' Jeb would explain. And indeed it was. He even had a fragile poster from 1892 announcing 'Whytteford Races' in bold letters. In years long past people had travelled from Salchester and Humbury to see the races at Whytteford. They had been proper races, not the type Old Harry and his friends had indulged in after school or when they climbed out of the windows when the schoolmaster wasn't looking. Old Harry and his chums would capture donkeys and race them for fun.

A clanking steamroller was used

At school Jeb had not been a scholar. He could read and write well enough; maths, other than basic arithmetic, was beyond him, but in art he excelled. He could draw and he could paint. His teacher told him about the great British artists, which paints they used and how their styles varied. Jeb discovered that colours such as vermilion, emerald green, chrome yellow, cobalt blue, lead white and madder were ground in a variety of mediums such as linseed oil mixed with pine resin. The artists of old had made their own paints, not bought them and squeezed them out of tubes.

With his knowledge and his natural skills Jeb could produce wonderful pictures of local scenes in the style of various artists. There was always a signature, as Jeb never claimed that the pictures were by famous painters as often they were of scenes that the artists of old had never visited. Occasionally the signature was a little vague but if you knew his work you saw that he had scrawled Jeb Carpenter in a flowing style. Jeb would spend winter evenings producing romanticised scenes of The Forest, so that in the summer they could be sold to delighted tourists seeking souvenirs.

'The Cobblers Arms' seemed an odd name as cobblers did not have coats of arms. Jeb investigated the history of the name and discovered why there was this unusual name for a public house. After the Whytte family had ceased to live at the manor it had been owned by the Grayville family and they were succeed by the Cobbleighs. In the 17th century The Cobbleigh Arms was quite popular but the broad dialect of The Forest resulted in changed pronunciation and everybody knew the hostelry as The Cobblers Arms. The name had stuck and remained in use long after the Cobbleighs had been forgotten. Anything ridiculous, spoken after someone had drunk too much ale, was consequently greeted with laughter and, 'What a lot of cobblers!'

In the summer Jeb also found time to run the Whytteford cricket team and although they were not the finest team in The Forest they often won matches against better sides because of Jeb's cunning. If the batting was not going well, he knew when to call a tea break, really an excuse for beer, as this might upset the bowlers of the opposing team. Jeb knew that one of the Whytteford bowlers was timid sober but a demon with the ball after two pints of ale, so he exploited that knowledge; often to great effect.

Although he was captain of the team, Jeb always allowed others to open an innings and usually listed himself as seventh or even eighth batsman. He was a strong and bulky man who preferred not to run too much. When it was time for him to bat he was in no rush to score as he allowed himself at least a couple of overs to assess a bowler's skill. In those overs Jeb would control the ball, hitting it low so that he would not be caught out. Occasionally a run might be scored but often spectators had to wait until Jeb had decided it was time for action. This meant that a ball suddenly went flying over the cricket field scoring four runs and often six. Opposition captains might reposition their fielders but that meant that Jeb struck the ball in a different direction, away from anyone's hopeful hands.

At one match the Whytteford team was twenty-three runs behind and there was only one over left in for the opposition to bowl. The sun was starting to give a golden glow to The Forest and swallows swooped over the field gathering insects on the wing. Jeb stood ready to receive what the bowler had to offer and with his unique style he crashed the ball across the field and scored twenty-four runs without ever leaving the crease! The opposing team, despondent after losing a match they looked sure to win, soon cheered up when Jeb bought them all some good ale. The swallows, oblivious of the drama that they had barely witnessed, twisted and dipped over the cricket field and caught the insects that were dancing in the light of the setting sun.

Perkins

Humbury was a remarkable little town that barely changed for decades. J.J. Swindles the undertakers had been there for a few generations. The small brewery, owned by Hornmans, produced ale for The Forest and their brewer's dray, pulled by two sturdy horses, plodded round the streets and along the lanes with casks carefully stacked. There were many traditional shops: milliners, family butchers with rabbits and pheasants hanging on display as well as venison sausages and wild game pies in the window, tailors that had been run by the same family for years, a fishing tackle shop, a gunsmiths, county outfitters, bakers where the smell of new bread seemed to permanently hover and most intriguingly the ironmongers.

The Perkins family had been ironmongers before Great-Grandpa George had moved his family to The Forest, and the stock reflected their history. Whatever you needed vaguely connected with ironmongery then you went to Perkins. You could buy one screw of a particular size or a whole boxful. If you had an outdated machine and needed a spare part, then Perkins would probably have it in stock. Outside the shop were exciting displays of tin baths, dustbins, brooms and mops, mole traps, parasols and wheelbarrows with a plethora of assorted equipment. The display never reflected the season and so sun beds and sledges were often together.

Outside the shop were exciting displays

51

Davey Perkins ruled his business in unique style. Time was of no importance to him, so in the afternoons the shop re-opened when he had woken from his lunchtime snooze. Often a queue of customers was waiting at two o'clock, but Davey made no apology if it was ten past two, or later, when he unlocked the door. He would then distribute the customers round the store.

'I need some paint brushes.'

'Over there, over there,' Davey would say, flapping his hand vaguely in the direction of where the brushes might be.

'Rat traps?'

'Down there, down there.'

'Preserving jars?'

'Up the top, there.'

'Lamp fittings?'

'Over there, over there.'

'Fire lighters.'

'Down on the left.'

'Creosote?'

'Out the back. Out the back.'

'Coach bolts?'

'Ah, I know where they are. Come with me.'

The wonderful thing about visiting Perkins was that you always left with a smile on your face. You might go to the counter with a collection of items and Davey added up the prices.

'Two fifty; two twenny - five; noinety pence; sixty-foive pence; three twenny. Call it noine pounds shall we?'

'That's very good of you.'

'That's all roight, sir. I'll charge the customer behind you'm a pound extra.' Comments like this were made straight-faced and so you smiled all the more.

New staff soon adopted the Perkins' style and humour abounded. A Sikh, complete with turban, joined the staff.

'Good afternoon, sir,' he would say in rich accent. 'And what can I be doing for you today?' And then he would add, in a totally different voice, 'Sorry about that, mate, but one has to adopt the Perkins' style!'

One customer was looking for vine eyes; handy gadgets that you can screw into a post and use for stretching wires upon which vines are grow. They have other uses as well.

'Do you have any vine eyes?'

'Certainly, sir. How many would you like?'

'A couple of dozen.'

"Vine eyes…mmm…… mmm. A moment later Davey was singing. 'Vine eyes have seen the glory of the coming of the Lord!'

As it was so unchanging Humbury gradually became a popular tourist town. Thursdays had always been the day for early closing and at one o'clock doors would be locked, blinds pulled down and all the shops would shut. Thursday visitors to the little town were disappointed, as they couldn't even have a lollipop as a treat. The shopkeepers began to realize that they were losing valuable business and early closing day became a thing of the past; visitors could buy ice cream, visit a tea room and buy souvenirs. Eventually every shop was open on 'early closing day' except one: Perkins! Davey saw no point. Why should his shop open for tourists? Local customers pointed out that they too visited Humbury on Thursdays and they expected the shop to be open. Grudgingly Davey decided that he would have to begin opening on Thursday afternoons and a sign appeared in the window. It was hand-written in large letters.

'From now on Perkins will be open on Thursday afternoons.'

But if you studied the sign carefully there was another sentence in much smaller letters. This read, 'As an experiment.'

Waiting to be served one day I heard a wonderful example of the humour that made Perkins special.

'My woife sayz I don't sleep.'

'Ah! Moine's the same. I dan't need to sleep.'

'I say that to 'er. I sayz I dan't wantta sleep.'

'Some people die in their sleep.'

'Ah! That's true.'

'If you'm dies when you're asleep you knaw what'll 'appen?'

'What'z that then?'

'You'll bloomin' miss it!'

A Knock At The Door

Many of the homes in Whytteford had antique pieces of furniture either clearly on display or tucked in corners. Many had been handed down through generations and few people had any idea of their true worth. Some of the antiques had been bought in house sales after the Second World War when so many of the great country houses were abandoned as the upkeep was too great. Villagers from The Forest had worked at Challington Manor and in other country houses or on the estates. After a long period of service valuable appreciations were often given; jewels, porcelain, pictures and occasionally fine items of furniture.

Tucked away in her little wattle and daub cottage Mrs Landy enjoyed her retirement. On the wall was a finely framed picture, a landscape with some deer grazing beneath impressive trees. In the distance, across the meadows, could be seen the spire of Salchester Cathedral. Mrs Landy explained to new visitors that it was valuable. Lady Dusbury had told her so when she presented the picture to Mrs Landy on her retirement after many years of faithful service. Mrs Landy also had a little chest that was finely carved and exquisitely decorated. It was very useful. In a pot in the top drawer Mrs Landy kept her change, so that there was always some money ready to pay the milkman and the baker.

Another item Mrs Landy was very proud of was a little metal dish. Lady Dusbury had also given that to her as a present on her sixtieth birthday. Mrs Landy often thought of the time she had worked for Lady Dusbury. They had got on well despite her ladyship's 'difficult' moments. Mrs Landy had dealt with those by remaining very calm and very quiet but also maintaining a sweet smile until her ladyship would burst out laughing and say, 'There I go again! What a silly old fool I am!' Then both of them would laugh and the matter would be forgotten. The metal dish was beautifully crafted and had a delicate decorative pattern. Underneath there was some curious lettering that Mrs Landy did not understand. Lady Dusbury had said it was Russian lettering.

Occasionally strangers would visit the village and knock on doors hoping to buy antique items at advantageous prices. They would then slip away before they became too well known. For professional reasons, and their own safety, these slippery characters never visited the village twice.

One afternoon, not long after lunch, there was a loud knock on the door of Mrs Landy's cottage.

'That's odd,' thought Mrs Landy, who was not expecting anyone to call, 'I wonder who that is? I don't know anyone who knocks like that.'

The knock had been so loud that she thought it sounded almost rude. Nevertheless Mrs Landy opened the door. Standing before her was a man who wanted to be seen as smartly dressed. He wore a dark pin-striped suit but it was rumpled and crumpled and past redemption. His shirt was a little frayed at the collar and his tie was too brash for Mrs Landy's liking. He also stood very close to the door.

'Good afternoon,' said the man in an oily manner. 'I wonder if you could help me. I have a problem with my car.'

'What's that then?'

'You see it's broken down. I think it just needs some water.'

'You can get that from the well, I'll fetch a jug for you.'

When Mrs Landy returned she was surprised to find the man had come into her little cottage and he was looking at her special picture.

'Here's the jug. You can fill it at the well and take it to your car.'

'What a beautiful picture.'

'Yes, I'm very fond of it.'

'Did you know it is quite valuable?'

'Is it really?'

'Oh yes, indeed. Have you had it long? Do you know anything about it?'

'It was given to me by Lady Dusbury from Challington Manor and she told me their family had owned it for nearly two hundred years.'

The stranger gave a little smile of delight that Mrs Landy did not miss even though it was hastily subdued.

'Really? How very interesting.'

'Why's that then?'

'Oh...I...dabble in these things. If you would like to sell it I could make you a very good offer.'

'It's not for sale. I'm very fond of that picture.'

'But it's so valuable. You would be so much better off.'

'Just a moment,' said Mrs Landy. 'I must turn the stove off in the kitchen.' She left the man for a moment, went into the kitchen and returned.

Across the meadows could be seen the spire of Salchester Cathedral

'It really is very old.' The man had now removed the picture from the wall and was examining the reverse side of the frame. He saw the crude nails that held the rough backing panel in place. He saw a once white label, now a brownish cream. There was a flamboyant signature with a large capital J and flourishing capital C. The signature even finished with what looked to be an extended flourish on an 'e'.

'Well, what would you offer me?'

The man suppressed another little smile. The picture would soon be his; all he needed to do was negotiate.

'Well…mmm… I think…seventeen fifty would be fair.'

'Do you now? You tell me it's old and valuable and then offer just seventeen fifty.'

'Age doesn't automatically mean *great* value,' the man replied smoothly.

'You might as well go, then.'

The man was shocked. He'd never had a reaction like that before.

'I might just stretch my offer a little.'

'I would have thought thirty-seven fifty would have been reasonable.'

'Madam, I am already being generous. Now here is my final offer. Twenty-seven fifty.'

At that moment there was another knock at Mrs Landy's door so she went to open it. There stood the huge figure of Jeb Carpenter, the energetic captain of the local cricket team. He was holding a pitchfork that had sharp and shining prongs.

'Hello, Ella,' he said in his loudest voice. "Ow are you?'

'Fine, Jeb. This man's just offered to buy my picture from me.'

"Ope you'm paying her well,' said Jeb, thrusting his face uncomfortably close to the man.

'Of… of… course.'

'What you'm payin' then?'

'He's offered twenty-seven fifty,' said Mrs Landy.

'Two thawsand seven 'undred and fifty pouns, that's a roight good affer.'

Suddenly the man was shaking.

'I meant twenty seven pounds fif—'

'Naw, come on 'n pay up. You'm made yer affer so don't try wrigglin' out of it,' said Jed with more than a hint of menace in his voice. He was also brandishing his pitchfork rather alarmingly.

His hands shaking, the man reached into his jacket and,

to the amazement of Jeb and Ella, produced a great bundle of greasy notes. Quivering, he counted out £2750 and put the notes on the table.

'Than...than... thank you,' he stammered. 'I must go now.' He was pale and visibly shaking as he held the picture tight and opened the door.

'Don't you'm come 'ere agin,' said Jeb, pointing with the pitchfork.

'Don't you need your water?' called Mrs Landy. But the man had gone.

Moments later Jeb looked out of the door; the stranger had vanished. Jeb went back into the cottage.

'I saw you'm put the red jug in the kitchen winda, Ella, so I knew to come.'

'Thank goodness you saw the signal. Thank you, Jeb.'

'Reckon you'm got a good price for that picture, don' you?'

'It works, every time doesn't it, Jeb?'

'Yeah, fun 'int it?'

'You are very clever with your paints and brushes.'

'And oi've got the right initials,' added Jeb Carpenter. 'Oi wonder if he'll check the signature. 'Slong as I's not too neat tis a job to tell whose it is.'

'Usual split then, Jeb?'

'That suit's me, Ella. Oi'll do another one for yer. What yer fancy this toime?'

'Another view of Salchester cathedral would be nice. After all, we know that John Constable painted it quite a lot of times.'

'That's roight, Ella. A little one turned up in a saleroom the other week.'

'Did he paint it, Jeb?'

'Well...that's what it said in the catalogue!'

Politics

The people of The Forest hardly dabbled in local politics. Life went on without the need for much political discussion as all the candidates were neighbours or friends. Local elections did happen but they seldom caused a ripple. Frank Midgley owned large orchards and everyone knew him as a fruit grower, which is what he was. He'd been a local councillor for years and was always re-elected until he made a simple mistake.

Local elections had come round again and as usual discussions among the men in The Cobblers Arms were about far more important things such as the yield of wheat per acre, which beer was best and wasn't Ebby Maybury's daughter, Bessie, shaping up very nicely. As usual a few candidates were standing for election but everyone expected Frank Midgley to win, and why not? He was a good reliable man.

But Frank made a big mistake. He gave himself airs. A new government at Whitehall was using all sorts of fancy titles dreamt up for old policies dressed as new and Frank decided that he must move with the times. On his application for election and the ballot papers he was no longer described as a fruit grower. Frank had decided he was an economist. He thought that would make an impression on people and show what a progressive and up-to-date fellow he was. In The Cobblers discussion was minimal.

'I see Frank's an eeconomist now.'

'No ee's not, ee's a fruit grower.'

'Anyway, what is an eeconomist when ee's about?'

'Reckon it's someone who wants to charge us more for less.'

'Wonder if Frank really knows what an eecony nommyist is?

'Ah. I saw Bessie'd got one of they tight jumpers on her today…'

'Must keep an eye open for that.'

And that was the end of the political discussion. Frank had lost the respect of the small electorate and he was never a councillor again.

General Elections were rather more exciting. Our sitting Member of Parliament was Sir Arthur Winsom-Wilde and he was hugely respected. The Forest was his first love and it could truly be said that The Forest without Sir Arthur would not have been The Forest. Shortish, comfortably rotund, with a round face topped by a mop of grey hair and large-framed glasses perched on a slightly hooked nose, Sir Arthur had the aura of a benign and rather dishevelled owl.

Everyone knew Sir Arthur and he treated all with equal friendship and courtesy. Election meetings held in Whytteford Village Hall were unusual as they were chaired by Silas Manston, an old fellow who had worked on the Winsome-Wilde estate all his working life and had known Sir Arthur almost from birth. As a result he referred to Sir Arthur as 'Mr Arthur' because old Silas had never called him anything else.

Sir Arthur had the aura of a benign and rather dishevelled owl

'I'd loike to welcome Mr Aarthur and thaank him for coming to see us this ev'nin',' he rumbled through his

61

limited teeth and shaggy moustache.

Sir Arthur would make his carefully prepared but seemingly spontaneous election address, then the meeting was open for questions.

'Who's got a question for Mr Arthur?'

'Sir Arthur, what views do you hold on the government's plans to pass a law restricting…'

'Well, Mr Arthur? Where do you stand on this?' Silas Manston seemed oblivious of the simple fact that he was the only person saying Mr Arthur. The meeting went on.

'I would like to ask Sir Arthur whether his party will protect farmers from…'

'Mr Arthur, do you have good news on this matter?'

Sir Arthur was very adept at answering any question and making everyone believe that what he said was right. Whichever way the election went nationally Sir Arthur held on to his seat. These meetings were good fun and despite the fact that this was a general election most questions were about local issues. After the meeting, which never lasted more than forty-five minutes, Sir Arthur would move on to another village hall where he gave exactly the same seemingly spontaneous speech and usually answered another variety of questions.

At one general election a rival candidate held his own meetings and tried to outdo Sir Arthur. Wherever he went his address was precisely the same; nothing wrong with that, it was just what Sir Arthur would do. Then there were questions from the audience. Word soon got about that the questions and answers were always identical as this clever fellow had a small group of supporters who travelled with him and tried to make life easy with their rehearsed questions, so that the candidate could give suitable answers. Sir Arthur was highly amused to learn of this tactic as he knew what the reaction would be, and he was right. His majority was bigger than ever and the clever rival lost his deposit.

Old Harry assured me that elections were dull compared

with when he was a lad. There was no radio or television in those days but there was great discussion in The Cobblers. When he was younger Harry and his friends used to have a way of adding a little spice to the proceedings. Harry's father had owned the local watermill and employed several staff and they found milling was thirsty work as their throats were parched by the flour dust. After work each day they would visit The Cobblers to slake their thirst and at the time of a general election discussion could get quite exciting.

Harry and his friends were adept at making stink bombs and also using them very cunningly. Early one evening the men from the flour mill were recovering in the bar when one of the election candidates called in. The discussion was totally amicable although hardly any of the men would vote for this man as they barely knew him.

The young Harry and his mates, watching from the nearby bridge, decided that here was a chance for some fun, especially as Harry knew that his father really disliked this political hopeful. Not wishing to draw attention to themselves they went to the back door of The Cobblers and slipped in.

'Where's Bob?' asked Harry. 'My dad needs Bob at the mill!' He looked around the men and as he did so his friends quietly slipped the stink bombs in between the boots of the drinkers. A moment later Harry and his friends had gone and were hidden in bushes near the bridge. The political discussion continued but soon the boots crushed the stink bombs, the bar emptied and the political discussion came to an abrupt halt.

'You ought to do summat loike that at an election do,' Harry said to me. 'Make it more interesting. I can still make the stink bombs when you need 'em!' He was a rogue but the most loveable rogue you could ever meet. 'And then,' he said, 'we used to start the fires…'

Cannon At The bridge

The approach to Challington Manor is across a little brick bridge beyond which is a gravel drive. Either side of some gates, pointing towards the bridge, are some historic cannon that one of Lord Dusbury's ancestors had rescued after some historic conflict and hidden them away. At the end of the nineteenth century the cannon had been uncovered from beneath decades of debris and put on display. They look rather impressive and make a suitable baronial statement suggesting the historical links of the Dusbury family.

Close inspection of the bridge reveals that the brickwork has some quite heavy damage on one side yet the other side of the bridge is in nearly perfect condition. Mosses and ivy decorate it and grasses grow close by. A clear stream flows over the gravel stones and often trout may be spotted among the waterweed. Why was the bridge damaged on just one side?

The cannon suggested the historical links of the Dusbury family

Old Harry always had tales to tell. He had been born in Whytteford and lived all his life there and he had seen the village gradually change. He knew all sorts of odds and ends about the local history; some of which were not common knowledge.

'Do you know anything about the bridge to the manor?' I

asked him.

'Whaaat d'you'm mean boi that?' he replied in his thick Forest accent.

'The bridge has some funny scars on one side. Do you know what caused them?'

'Ah...matterovfact I doz.'

'Could you tell me about it?'

'S'pose oi could now. Affer all it'appened long toime ago.'

I felt a shiver of excitement as this promised to be a good story.

'You'm know them cannon t'oither side ov the bridge, eh?'

'Yes, they're rather fine.'

'S'right. Well...my friends a oi decoided to test one ov'em.'

'Really? That must have been exciting.'

'Carse it woz, but don'you'm go gettin' idearz,' said Harry. 'Carse in them dayz you'm could boiy all you'm needed to make foirewarks. Cas'n boiy the stoff neow. Good thing too.'

It was autumn and Harry and his mates had been busy preparing for November 5th. They had created their own fireworks but had some gunpowder left over. Someone had the bright idea of testing one of the cannon at Challington Manor and that's when the fun began.

The boys gathered up old rags, odd pieces of iron, rusty nails and bolts and anything else they could muster for ammunition. One evening, when the sun had set and twilight had given way to darkness, they met in the woods opposite the manor. The boys had planned their scheme well; carefully thinking about what to do if anyone approached whilst they were at work. The moment a sound was heard they would dive down close beside the cannon and keep still until the danger had passed. First they had cleared the way for the fuse with a length of wire and then they inserted their fuse; a length of string soaked in paraffin and melted candle wax. Two at time they gathered at the cannon and pushed in gunpowder, wadding made from old rags, chunks of metal, round stones, and then some more wadding. They tapped it all home using a broom handle with a disc of wood nailed to it. And then the cannon was ready to fire.

'We waz all 'idden behind them bushes on th'other soide of the road,' explained Harry. 'We'm was trying to decoide who should loight the fuze, coz we had'n thawt abart it.'

'Who did it then?'

'Oi did ov carse. Then they could'st orl blame me iftit went wrang! I wen'over to the bridge, knelt besoide the cannon and lit t'fuse. Then oi scappered back to'm bushes. Momen' later there was this flazsh'nbang and the cannon shart all the odds'nendz straight owt'is maouth!'

'Wow! That must have been something to see.'

'Carse t'was. We orl ran loike the blazes carse the boom woz so lowd! You'm see we warn't gonna be caught. Nex' day uz all crept back to see wha'd 'appened. Bridge waz still there but there were orl these chunks missin'. Cannon had been pointin' straight at the bridge 'n we 'ad'nt noticed.'

'What did you do?'

'Nothin' we could do excep' put mud on the bridge where we'd foired at it and hittit!'

'Were you ever found out?'

'Naw. We niver told nawbody. Matter've fact, you'm the foirst person oi've ever told abart it. That waz a larng toime ago, so oi don' think oi'll get into trouble.' He gave a rich laugh. 'Carse you'm granfer didn'ave anythin' to do with all thart! 'Ee always kept art ov trouble and oi waz always getting' into it!'

Dandelion Wine

When the dandelions were in full bloom it was time to make wine! In April and May many villagers would gather dandelions and begin brewing their country wine. The process was quite simple and many claimed that dandelions made the finest rustic wine.

Large containers would be filled with the bright flower heads, then boiling water was added and the mixture left alone for a couple of days; an occasional stir being the only attention required. Next everything was poured in to a huge saucepan together with more water, juice and zest from lemons, a lot of sugar and crushed raisins. The mixture was boiled until bubbling then left to simmer for a while. Recipes varied. Some people included orange juice; some put in a touch of ginger. Most people made sure all stalks were excluded as they had a bitter taste but others included some stalks to make a drier wine.

When the dandelions were in full bloom it was time to make wine!

Various other wines were made. Elderflower, which was pale and delicate; elderberry, which was rich; gooseberry, which varied according to who made it and even parsnip wine, which looked like pale amber, was specially favoured. In times past cowslips were in abundance and so cowslip wine was created as well. Some of these wines were gently fortified with 'secret' additions distilled furtively in outhouses. A sparkling wine for special occasions was rhubarb champagne; which had a special flavour that had hints of neither rhubarb nor champagne. The after effects could be curious. In contrast sweet onion wine had a bouquet that gave no doubt about the wine's origins.

Some villagers ventured on to more exotic things gathering birch, sloes and rosehips. The oddest creation was a supposedly delicious 'sherry' made from banana skins. It had the right colour but a unique flavour that meant once tasted the 'sherry' was never forgotten and always avoided.

Certain of the concoctions produced unexpected and unwanted consequences. A batch of birch wine, for some reason a curious shade of green, was reputed to have caused momentary lockjaw that lasted at least thirty seconds and if a large glass had been drunk too rapidly rendered the drinker speechless for several minutes. The fizzy rhubarb wine could have sudden consequences and onion wine could be quite antisocial in at least two respects. Never kiss anyone who has just had a glass of onion wine! Mrs Sponder created birch and gooseberry wine. An unusual combination, each flavour supposedly complimenting the other, but one year the consequence of drinking this alcoholic creation was green teeth. Eventually the discolouration faded but the tart acidity lingered on.

But amongst all these intriguing creations dandelion wine was king. The ingredients were easily gathered, the process was simple and the fermentation period reasonably brief. The results could be a clear yellowy amber wine that looked delicious. Yet even this locally famous wine could have its drawbacks. Recipes varied and certain ingredients could cause surprises. One unfortunate batch was reputed to cause icy sensations on the hottest summer day. A chill spread from the tongue and gradually took over the entire mouth, teeth became chilled and fillings began to throb.

In late July each year the Whytteford Village Show took

place. There were competition classes for flowers, vegetables, summer fruits, country wines and other rural produce. Wines of rainbow flavours appeared but the largest contingent amongst the alcoholic beverages was the wondrous dandelion wine. The clear glass bottles were lined up with labels and numbers to the front. No makers' names were on display; the judges had no idea who had created each bottle. It was interesting to see so many bottles of what was supposedly the same wine. Colours ranged from a rich amber through liquid gold to the palest primrose yellow. The judges sampled each bottle taking little sips and savouring the best wines and rejecting the less successful offerings. One year, at bottle number eleven, the adjudication came to a halt as the judges each developed a coughing fit that they could not control. They had struck an especially dry version of dandelion wine. But more drama was yet to come.

There had been twenty-three offerings of dandelion wine for the judges to taste. Once they had recovered from the coughing fit the judging recommenced. After tasting twenty mediocre samples and one immediate reject, they encountered something special; a bottle of light amber perfection that was not too dry and had a light flowery taste and earthy richness. Here was the winner! Number twenty-two was a fine wine and the judges showed their appreciation in no uncertain terms. When they had completed their task the bottle was virtually empty.

But their selection, whilst undoubtedly fair and right, caused controversy. The maker lived in the village; she had picked her dandelions in the village and she had used all the normal ingredients for dandelion wine, although the proportions may have been different. There was no secret about this wine as it was just a bottle of country wine. What could be controversial about it? The maker. She was new to Whytteford and had never made this wine before. Wanting to become involved in village life she had made her wine and entered a sample bottle at the Village Show and won. A newcomer who a few months before had not known that wine could be created from dandelions had trumped old men and women who had made dandelion wine for decades.

Many people asked, 'Who gave you the recipe?'

'Nobody,' the lady replied. 'I found it in a book.'

This caused much mystification and head shaking. A dandelion wine recipe from a book? Such a thing was unheard of. Nobody knew such books existed.

'How did you get it *so* clear?'

'I followed the recipe very carefully.'

This lead to more head shaking and puzzlement and some entrants felt that this lady had 'cheated' but admitted that they couldn't fault anything that she had done.

A year passed.

Would this lady win the wine competition again?

She didn't make any wine.

Having achieved victory she moved on to something else, entered the cake competition and, to the disgust of many, won that instead.

Nuns In The Distance

Across the common, where The Forest met the fields and farms, there was a nunnery. The nuns were kept busy running a small mixed farm. From the distance the scene looked rather quaint and almost from another century. The nuns, dressed in blue habits with white wimples, worked the fields attending to the animals, tilling the earth, sowing seed and gathering crops. The illusion was somewhat distorted when one saw a nun, still wearing her habit and wimple, driving a tractor.

Closer encounters brought reality to the fore and the romantic illusion was totally shattered. The blue habits were usually torn and grubby, especially around the hems, and the wimples were far from white. To see the nuns going about their farm work from the distance was best as then the Wellington boots, worn for most of the year, were not seen protruding below the habits.

The worst time to pass Nunnery Farm was around milking time. The nuns drove the cows from field to milking parlour often crossing a lane in the process. They wielded long stout sticks that they used to goad and steer cows in the right direction. Any beast wandering off the wrong way was given a sharp thwack with a nun's stick to put it back on course. The thwack was usually accompanied by unusual comments that the cows failed to appreciate.

'Daisy, you old mucker, if you don't do as you're told you'll be saying Hail Mary seven times before the evening's out!'

'Don't you lift your tail to me, Mirabelle! I don't want your shite over me!'

The nuns in charge of the cows seemed to have a hard time and their dirty habits often had a certain odour about them. If the cows and nuns were crossing the road a vehicle had no chance of getting through.

'If you don't move on Patsy I'll set the Devil on your tail; indeed I will!'

The cows would just stare dolefully at the nuns and plod on, their full udders swaying beneath them. Somehow the idyllic scenes of the distance were viewed differently after such close encounters.

Nuns were viewed differently after close encounters

Occasionally one would see a nun in a creamy white habit and wimple. They didn't work in the fields but would be seen walking about the farm locality on dry paths. These were the nuns who were about to take their final vows and devote themselves to God. Even at the age of twelve I noticed that some of these supposedly supremely devoted nuns were very pretty.

From our home you could walk easily to two post boxes. One was not far but meant walking on the lanes. The other, close to the nunnery, was further but the walk, in good weather was delightful. I would set out across the common, enjoying the views and looking for wild life. Some of the pathway was through woodland and was a good spot to look out for foxes, especially in the spring when the young cubs could often be seen at play. I used to move as silently as possible, taking my time, and if there was a glimpse of fox, badger, deer, pheasant or partridge I would freeze and then try and creep slowly and silently closer.

One warm afternoon I was moving soundlessly along the path and as I came round some bushes where the path took a turning I saw something I had never seen before. There was a nun, in creamy white habit, clasped in a passionate embrace with a man. They certainly had not heard my approach, but the moment I was seen they split apart. She was very pretty with a flushed face and sparkling blue eyes that I can remember to this day. I silently swept past and went on to post my letter. What should I do now? Should I return along the path, possibly causing further embarrassment? No such thought passed through my mind. As I walked back I was hoping to see more of this unusual meeting but the two lovers had gone their separate ways.

On my return home I told my parents about the scene I had so briefly witnessed.

'Where was this?' asked my father.

'At the woods not very far from the post box.'

'Are you sure she was a nun?' asked my mother.

'Of course I am.'

'I wonder if he'll get in the habit,' muttered my father. My mother immediately reprimanded him but she was stifling a giggle.

Nothing more was said but when I left the kitchen a few moments later I heard guffaws of laughter.

That evening visitors came to see my parents. Suddenly there was some loud laughter followed by, 'It's surprising what the nuns get up to!' spoken too loudly. 'Hush, Cyril! That's enough!' lead to even more laughter.

I often wondered what happened to that nun. Did she take her final vows? Could she take her final vows? A few years later I was in Humbury and a pretty lady with sparkling blue eyes was there, pushing a pram. Perhaps she was the passionate nun. I hope so. Those blue eyes seemed familiar and were unforgettable.

Such Exotic Fauna

The Forest was a popular destination for tourists. Many came from cities and towns for a weekend in the countryside and they'd be in such abundance it was as if a swarm had arrived.

'Lot've grockles about,' was often muttered in The Cobblers Arms as another party of strangers arrived.

The landlord at The Duck and Monkey at Breamhill even had a 'grockle count' meter on display that was adjusted every day as the tourists flooded The Forest.

Old Harry always called them emmets as they came in swarms. 'Loike emmets,' he'd say. 'Jus' loike them emmets.'

Having a field to spare we occasionally had tourists with caravans visiting. Many would return as they had discovered a quiet spot where the sun usually seemed to shine. One regular visitor always wore the jolliest clothes. He might be dressed in blue and white-banded shirt, bright red trousers and a red cap at a jaunty angle. He was always smiling, always happy and certainly relished his visits to The Forest.

'You see,' he explained, 'being here is so different from my work. I'm an undertaker.'

For some grockles country life was a whole new experience.

'I couldn't get to sleep, it was so quiet,' was quite a regular comment.

Woodpeckers were common birds to us; we saw them almost every day. The red fox was often seen at dusk or early in the morning and really caused little trouble provided people kept their hens and ducks secure. Adders were often to be seen basking in the sun, tucked away in the heather and gorse. They are really shy creatures that don't want to be disturbed and they do not attack unless they feel threatened. If you think there might be adders about stamp your feet and they will soon make themselves scarce. People are frightened of them but in fact wasp and bee stings cause more deaths than adder bites.

The grockles were not used to the wild life that the inhabitants of The Forest regarded as perfectly normal.

'You do get some strange birds here. Have they flown in from the continent?'

'What have you seen?'

'We saw one that was black and white with a red head and some red under the tail. Very odd, it was. We've never seen anything like it.'

'That was probably a woodpecker.'

'Are they rare?'

'Not here.'

As well as the Great Spotted Woodpecker the Green Woodpecker was common too. With its green and yellow plumage and a red head this woodpecker has a very striking appearance and it also gives a distinct call. The flash of colours and its clear cry constantly amazed visitors. Something we took for granted was a source of amazement.

'I'm sure I saw a bird from Africa,' one lady said.

'She must be right,' agreed her husband. 'You don't get birds like that in this country.'

Pheasants and partridges were regularly seen wandering around The Forest, especially where there was free food for them.

'I saw a big bird with a long tail,' the visitors might say.

'Probably a pheasant.'

'Oh, that's what a pheasant looks like. I've eaten them but I didn't know they looked like that.'

One visitor was in a state of real distress. He was a Cockney who had seldom ventured out of London.

'I opened the caravan door this morning and saw a great big creature coming out from the trees. Has something escaped from a zoo? I was so frightened.' There was a tremor in his voice as he spoke.

'Did it attack you?'

'It didn't have a chance. I slammed the door shut.'

'What did it do then?'

'It just slipped by and into the bushes. I told Mavis to

stay in. Do you think it was dangerous? Will it be about again?' The poor man's hands were shaking; he was really frightened.

'What colour was it?'

'It was rusty red and had a huge tail, a really huuuge tail.'

'I expect it was a fox. They have big bushy tails. It won't come into your caravan.'

What else could be said? We didn't dare to mention the adders.

We didn't dare to mention the adders

Christmas Trees

When we planted the Christmas trees they were just little saplings but they seemed to like the sandy soil of that part of The Forest. The trees put down their roots and gradually overcame the heather, bracken and gorse that grew amongst them. Occasionally we rough cut between the trees to give them space and air but mostly they fought their own battle against the other plants. Some birch trees managed to self-seed in between the Christmas trees but we left them to grow as they added colour and variety. Many of the trees were soon three to four feet high. Some scarcely seemed to grow but others romped away and swamped the weaker ones that eventually gave up the battle or tried to look like proper trees, but instead had the appearance of nature's rejects.

One cold December afternoon, not long before Christmas, it was time to select and cut a tree for our home. I put on my Wellington boots and a warm coat, picked up a bow saw and made my way across the lawns, through a small wood and on to where the Christmas trees were planted. As I began to select a tree I heard the sound of a van or truck stopping close by. At that moment I didn't think anything of it and went on looking for a tree. We wanted quite a tall one and I went further in to the plantation. Suddenly I realized that I was not alone. Out of view but only a few trees away someone was doing some sawing and it wasn't difficult to guess what was being cut. I quietly made my way through the Christmas trees ducking low to avoid the branches. Over a dozen trees had been sawn off and they were neatly bundled and stacked, ready to be transported. Using a billhook, an unshaven figure with wavy, greasy black hair, was deftly removing any straggly or dead branches from a tree. He was concentrating on his work and at first didn't notice me. Suddenly he looked up.

' 'Ello, mate,' he said calmly. 'You arfer one too?'

'That's right.'

'Yer can'ave one of these 'fyou likes. Save yer cutting 'im. A tenner to yer mate.'

'Thanks. I think I'll cut my own.'

' 'Im up at th'ouse is art,' he added. 'Saw'm go. So sis safe fer yer.'

'I know he's out. I saw him leave too.'

'S'all roight then. 'Elp yerself'n.'

That was quite an invitation. I was being told to help myself to Christmas trees planted on our own land.

I could see that our visitor had selected some of the best Christmas trees to take away. Eventually I found one nearly seven feet high and well branched that would fit in to the corner of the lounge. I trimmed off some scraggy lower branches then knelt down and cut through the trunk with the bow saw. The blade was sharp; it slid through the wood quite easily and after a few minutes of steady sawing the tree toppled a little. It did not fall over as surrounding trees supported it. I tidied up the base of the trunk, cut out a few dead twigs and began to pull the Christmas tree out of the plantation.

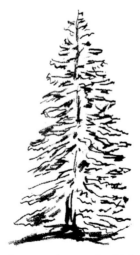

Eventually I found one nearly seven feet high and well branched that would fit in to the corner of the lounge

The intruder was hacking some rough branches from another tree that he had just cut. He looked at the tree that I had selected.

'You'm go a good'un thar.'

'It'll suit us.'

'Better get away. Cos 'im upatouse mi' be backs'n.' This man ran words together. I had to listen carefully to make out what he meant.

'Right, I'll be on my way.'

'Gi'us an'and to get these totruck.'

'Cheeky fellow,' I thought. But then it crossed my mind that if I helped him I might see the registration number on his truck. 'Certainly. I've got a few minutes to spare.'

Together we heaved twenty trees away from the plantation to the gate close by a forest track. Tucked away beneath an old oak was a dirty blue truck. The number plate was so muddy the letters and figures were indistinct. My efforts had been in vain. The intruder would make off with the trees and sell them for ten or more pounds each. For very little work he would make about two hundred pounds.

'Where will you be selling them?' I asked.

'Ah…er…'ere an'there.'

'Will you now,' said a firm voice that I knew well. Just behind an old oak was my father and when I looked to where the track joined the road I could see his Land Rover blocking the exit.

"Spose you'm calledpolis,' our visitor mumbled.

'Not yet. I can call them if you wish.'

'Nah. Misser. I'll pay yer for'emtrees. Fair'nsquare. Twenny quid.'

'You'll have to do better than that. I think five pounds a tree would be fair and square.'

'T'int got tha'much onme.'

'I'm not moving my vehicle for less.'

He was trapped and he knew it. I also noticed that his bronzed face was now a curious shade of grey. He was rattled and the colour had drained from his cheeks.

"S'alright then. You win.' He pulled a scruffy old wallet, stuffed with notes, from his jacket and took out a hundred pounds; without saying a word he thrust the notes into my father's hands. Ten-pound notes were rare in those days and five-pound notes were not common and so my father was paid in well-worn, greasy, green one-pound notes.

The man's hands were shaking and it was clear he couldn't wait to get away. Taking his time my father wandered to his Land Rover then turned to me. 'We might as well take our tree. Have you cut it?'

'Yes, I'll fetch it.'

I went back over the gate.

'C'mon mister! I gotta go,' said the man.

I collected our tree, we threw it up on to the back of the Land Rover and gently pulled away. A moment later the dirty blue truck, belching smoke and roaring like an angry ogre shot from its parking place, scattering turf and leaves in all directions. The driver stared straight ahead as he passed us and the truck lurched towards Humbury almost hidden by a cloud of foul exhaust fumes.

Chicken Problems

Gerry Mottstone owned many chicken. A variety of breeds made passing his farm quite a colourful experience. Plymouth Rocks mixed with Delawares and Buff Orpingtons and cockerels had flamboyant plumage that caught the eye. They were truly free-range hens that ran about his farmyard, into the fields, along the tracks and also on to the roads. Many people bought very fresh eggs from him as they really did have a better taste. Gerry had no problem with foxes as his dogs would keep guard during the day and the hens were well secured in hutches at night.

Humans were a bigger problem than any wildlife. Gerry lived close to the highway, which was normally quiet but could also have its busy times. Over the years the traffic slowly built up and eventually there were so many heavy lorries that the chicken lived in permanent danger. The vehicles were so massive that the drivers seldom spotted the chicken from their cabs. Traffic became steady and so fast that the free-range chicken were being run over at a rate of three to six a week.

Gerry found this very distressing, as he had no desire to restrict his hens. 'They'm free-range and that's 'ow they're to be!' he declared. Summer time, when tourists with their caravans flocked to the forest, could be especially dangerous as the drivers, concentrating on keeping vehicles and vans under control, barely noticed the hens as they pecked and clucked away next to the road.

Gerry called in at the police station in Humbury to complain.

'You've got to do something about all these people driving so fast and killing all my chickenses,' he said to the police   officer.
'What do you want me to do?' asked the policeman.

'I don't care, just do something about them crazy drivers!' As Gerry's farm wasn't too far from the village school a sign was erected that read:

CHILDREN CROSSING

For about a week this had some effect but once everyone was used to it the sign made no difference, especially during the school holidays.

Gerry decided another visit to the police was needed. On Market Day he called again at the Humbury Police Station.

'You've still got to do something about these drivers. The 'Children Crossing' sign seems to make them go even faster!'

After much consultation and officialdom a different sign appeared:

SLOW: CHILDREN AT PLAY

That really sped them up. Gerry called again at Humbury Police Station.

'That sign is no good. Can I put up my own sign?'

In order to get Gerry off his back the policeman said, 'Sure. Put up your own sign. Just make sure it's polite.' Gerry's visits to the Police Station stopped, but curiosity got the better of the officer, so he called Gerry.

'How's the problem with the speeding drivers. Did you put up your sign?'

'Oh, I sure did and not one chicken has been killed for weeks now.'

Naturally the policeman was really curious and thought he'd better take a look at the sign. He also thought the sign might be something the police could use elsewhere, to slow drivers down.

He drove out along the road close to Gerry's farmhouse and as he approached he saw a large clear sign. His jaw dropped in amazement as he read:

NUDIST COLONY
Slow down and watch out for chicks.

Slow down and watch out for chicks.

Cricket Matches

I have never had any skill at sport. My coordination for hitting balls with, bat, racquet, hockey stick or any other weapon has never been good. Curiously I used to know all the rules and umpires' signals for cricket. This came about one summer as a result of a series of wet afternoons that, much to my delight, meant we were unable to have any games sessions. Our cricket-mad games master was not going to waste our time by allowing us to read or revise for our forthcoming examinations. This was his time for sport and he was going to use it.

Using special dice, we created imaginary games of cricket. I can only recall that scores were accumulated according to how the die landed and that the bowler had his own die and the type of ball bowled depended on what he managed to throw. Now there came the clever part of this entertainment. We were all taught to be umpires and had to signal what was happening in this curious version of the game. If a 'six' was scored, pairs of hands shot up into the air. If there was a wide, arms stretched until we had to take care not to poke out another umpire's eye. No-balls, byes, leg byes and all the other cricket complexities were signalled in remarkable unison. After several weeks we were all expert umpires but one of us was still the most inept cricketer The Forest or the county had ever known.

Years later I let slip that I knew how to umpire a cricket match and I was soon involved with the local team. Jeb Carpenter was the captain of a typical Forest cricket team that ranged in age from 14 to 74. Jeb was very keen for there to be practice sessions but some of the team thought practice should last half an hour before there was a break, after which the practice continued in The Cobblers Arms. Some of the cricketers had unique styles of play that were just about acceptable in a Forest match but wouldn't be recognized at a different level.

Unfortunately Jeb failed to accept that umpiring was the

limit of my cricketing skills.

'Now tharn,' he said, 'you been to school, you been to carlege, you must be pretty skillful at the game.'

'No, Jeb,' I said, trying to sound firm, 'I'm really not up to it. I seldom hit the ball.'

'What's spoint ov arll that time at school and carlege if you can't play cricket? Call that an eddication?'

'I am always happy to umpire, but you'd be scraping beyond the bottom of the barrel if you needed me to play.'

'You never, knaw! We moight be glad ove yer one foine day.'

I hardly dared mention that my umpiring knowledge had been gained on wet days.

Most of the pitches in The Forest were on open land where ponies, donkeys, sheep and cattle roamed freely. There was always the sacred square in the middle protected by temporary fencing to keep the animals away but this didn't prevent the rabbits from keeping the grass trimmed. Forest cricket pitches certainly had individual qualities seldom found elsewhere. Batsmen who struck sixes freely were not always popular as some of the pitches were close to many gorse bushes and retrieving the ball could be a painful experience. Often the fielder could see the ball but was unable to reach it without the aid of a bat or some other useful implement. Umpiring at Chamford on one occasion I was intrigued to see the home team had a rake prominently in view.

'What's the rake for?' I asked my fellow umpire.

'You'll see soon enough,' he replied, then added in a lugubrious tone, 'probably in the third over.'

And in the third over the star batsman of the home team found form and sent the ball sailing into the gorse. Out came the rake and after some searching, swearing and raking the ball was recovered and the game continued.

The inevitable happened on a sunny Wednesday evening match at Breamhill. The animals had been driven from the pitch and the game was well under way. I was quite enjoying umpiring in this pleasant setting. The Breamhill team had scored 72 and the last ball of the final over before the tea break was being bowled. The number eight player from Breamhill struck the ball and it sailed into the air. One of the Whytteford team moved backwards, caught the ball and then stumbled. His foot had slipped into a rabbit hole. The teams went off for the tea break—really a beer break as the local pub always provided refreshments—and I thought little about what had happened. Suddenly Jeb was at my side.

A sunny Wednesday evening match at Breamhill

'You'm 'ave to bat fur uz,' he muttered. 'Jonah's twisted 'is ankle. Can't walk.'

'But... but...'

'I'll put yer larst, then you probably won' be needed,' he added consolingly.

'But I haven't touched a cricket bat for seven years.'

'Yer'l be foin.'

By the last over of the game Whytteford had reached

87

seventy with only six wickets lost, so I continued umpiring feeling safe. Unfortunately the next three balls resulted in three wickets being taken. The Breamhill team members were smiling confidently and I was quietly shaking. Three balls to go and the world's least competent cricketer was required to bat against a bowler who looked twice my size and six times my strength. His run up to the wicket resembled the gallop of a powerful carthorse and then, with a massive grunt, he launched his missile at me. I held my bat in a defensive position, not moving it, as I had no idea what to do. There was a mighty crack as the ball crashed into the bat then spun away.

'Yes!' bellowed Reg, my fellow batsman, confusing the Breamhill team and me. We ran and although they tried to run me out some fumbling of the ball meant I was at the other end of the wicket before the ball arrived. At least I was no longer facing the carthorse. I stood, ready to run should the need arise. After all we needed just two more runs to win and there were two balls to be bowled.

'Play!' shouted the umpire.

The carthorse galloped up, snorted and fired his missile.

Reg stood prepared to strike. The carthorse did not frighten him. With the eye of an expert and the stroke a man familiar with a rip-hook, he belted the ball across the pitch into the gorse bushes.

'Four!' bellowed the umpire.

Whytteford had won! I heaved a sigh of relief, my innings was over and I had faced just one ball bowled by the carthorse.

And that's how I achieved my highest ever score in a cricket game. The scorebook recorded against my name: '1 - not out!'

The Harshest Winter

Early one December the harshest winter for decades hit the country and even the most sheltered parts of The Forest did not escape the frost's icy fingers. A few clear and bitter nights decorated trees and bushes with frost and the days were so still and cold that barely any thaw could happen. The ancient tiny church, tucked in a quiet valley, was white-robed and gravestones stood out from the frosty grasses.

On the Sunday before Christmas the church was in festive state for the annual carol service. The path from the lych gate was slippery until the verger spread some ash and hung lanterns from the trees to guide the congregation. The tortoise stove had been lit early in the day to try and raise the temperature but to little effect. Everybody arrived well wrapped against the cold. Elderly ladies clung to each other as they struggled up the frozen path. Once inside the church they felt safe, settled into the old pews and admired the decorative greenery. Even the eagle on the lectern had a twist of ivy round its neck and carried a sprig of holly in its beak. The ancient harmonium had been polished and Mrs Sponder was making it wheeze through festive church melodies. To be honest I never knew what she was playing as Mrs Sponder had the gift of making every hymn sound exactly the same. Fortunately the rector had a good voice and led the congregation through every hymn regardless of the wheezes and groans that emanated from the harmonium.

The rector had asked me to read one of the lessons at the carol service. The ignorance of youth being on my side, I did not suffer from nerves beforehand. I practised before the service and during the final verse of the preceding carol strode up to the eagle lectern. I found my place in the huge Bible, grasped the great bird with both hands and began to read. Suddenly, part way through the reading, nerves struck and I gripped the eagle even more tightly. The wretched thing began to fly about in front of me and I had to concentrate to get to the final sentence. 'Thanks be to God,' were my final words and never before or since have they been said with such emphasis.

But my ordeal was not quite over. I returned to my pew as the rector announced the next carol, 'While shepherds watched their flocks by night.'

The vast Miss Sponder heaved her bulk back into place on the ancient harmonium. As she pumped with her feet and played with her fingers, something approximating to the right tune was squeezed out of it and we began to sing. Relief that my reading was over flooded through me and I sang with gusto. It would have helped if I had sung the right words but my mind had somehow linked in to the playground version.

'While shepherds washed their socks by night
All seated round the tub,
The angel of the lord came down
And they began...'

My mother gave me a strong nudge in the ribs and I fell silent.

As we left the church the jovial rector said, 'Thank you for a lovely reading you always make things interesting.'

The bitter nights and chilly days continued. On Christmas morning the ground, already hard, was covered in thick white hoar frost. Bushes and trees were decorated with white rhyme and water froze deep in the pools and lakes. The shallows of the rivers and streams were iced over and the fish hid down in the depths.

Church on Christmas morning was chillier than at the carol service and although the old tortoise stove had been lit the night before only the members of the congregation who sat close by felt any benefit. The rest of us, well protected with overcoats, scarves and gloves, prayed fervently for a short service as wisps of cold water vapour came from our mouths. The harmonium, creaking under the bulk of Mrs Sponder, struggled to respond to her vigorous footwork and puffed or coughed its way through the carols. The rector was well wrapped in his vestments and cloak but he must have been relieved to announce the final carol 'O Come all ye Faithful'. To be honest I was not feeling very faithful that morning and my dubious beliefs were distinctly veering towards the freedom of being an atheist and staying in a warm house.

That night the snow came and on Boxing Day the scenes in The Forest took on a spectacular beauty. For five nights the frost froze the snow, then on New Year's Eve a blizzard swept through that piled snow on top of frozen snow. The frost persisted for weeks and the snow was frozen to the ground.

The Forest wild life became adventurous searching for food. Foxes seldom seen in some parts scavenged round bins, desperate for any food. The deer, usually so shy that for many people they are invisible, ventured to the villages and close-by byres seeking food. They pawed the ground searching for moss beneath the hardened snow. Sympathetic farmers even put out hay for the deer, as fortunately the previous summer had been generous and there were ample supplies. Tramps gathered together in semi-derelict cottages, lit huge fires and sought food wherever any might be given.

At night the clear and frosty air seemed to make the stars shine with special brilliance. Our house was isolated and surrounded by open grass, now covered in snow. One especially clear and bitter night we heard a mysterious sound. It was a regular muffled clanking that carried across the open space and amplified itself as it bounced from the wall of the house. 'Clank,…clank…clank.' Then it would stop, there would be a faint rattling and the clanking would begin again. 'Clank…clank…clank, rattle, clank…clank.' What could it be? We switched off the lights, drew back the curtains and tried to peer out. The windows were thick with frost and so with some effort we opened up and stared across the moonlit snow. Several fallow deer were pawing the ground in their urge to find food but they made no noise. The clanking and rattling had now stopped. We closed the window, drew the curtains and then warmed ourselves by the roaring log fire.

Night after night the clanking and rattling came and went. What or who could be making this strange and rather spooky noise? The footprints outside gave no clues as the many deer had trampled the snow. One night I went to bed later than everyone else. Suddenly I heard it again. 'Clank…clank…clank.' The noise was right beneath my bedroom window. Determined to discover the source of this ghostly noise, I drew back the curtains and softly opened the window. Deer were below me pawing the ground. As I peered out one moved. 'Clank…clank…rattle.' This poor creature was suffering in a poacher's snare. A cruel slip noose round its neck had rubbed the hide raw. There was a wire that went down to a tin can. One foot of this tortured animal was caught in the can and as it moved the eerie clanking and rattling echoed through the winter night air. The mystery solved I settled in bed pondering on the needless cruelty a beautiful fallow deer had endured. Next day my father, with one carefully aimed shot, ensured that the poor creature's misery was over. With that horrible noose the deer was soon found as it could not stray far.

At Stanmoor Pool the water froze deeply making it almost solid. One night, when the moon was shining and its light was reflected by the white landscape, the message spread round the village youngsters, 'Come to Stanmoor!' and that's where we all went, some with skates, and some with walking sticks 'borrowed' from grandparents. We were all wrapped in extra layers with hats, scarves and gloves. Nobody brought a torch as the moon shining on the white ground lit the way. At the pool a fire was blazing on the bank and many young couples cuddled to keep each other warm.

*The moon was shining and its light was reflected
by the white landscape*

On the ice a rustic game of ice hockey was being played with a flat pebble swishing across the ice struck by hockey sticks, walking sticks and even old pieces of summer-hardened gorse. Those on skates glided across the ice their shadows dancing around them, sticks at the ready as the stone puck whizzed hither and thither with splendid rapidity that kept every player alert. Collisions galore resulted in no broken limbs as every player was layered with coats and several pairs of trousers, so that they just fell over laughing, picked themselves up and played on. Midnight came but who cared? The fire was burning brightly, the amorous couples warmed each other and the rustic game of ice hockey warmed everyone else. Someone produced a box of fireworks and set them off. They seemed brighter and more colourful than usual in that cold crisp and miraculously clear air. Great fountains of golden showers soared into the dark sky, and then a sharp bang was followed by a cascade of stars in a kaleidoscope of wonderful colour. That was a winter night that we would all remember, as it was probably a rare once-in-a-lifetime experience.

Steam And Diesel

A railway line ran through The Forest. It was quite busy as it connected Salchester to Humbury and Boshampton. Each station had its own goods shed and most deliveries to the area came by rail. Once a day an Victorian steam locomotive pulled the local goods train along the line dropping wagons off at the various villages. At Deanbury there would be great sacks of flour delivered to the bakery; some coal for Chamford; timber for another station; ironmongery, building supplies, wood for coffins, bolts of cloth and all manner of things for Humbury. Every day a little truck went from Humbury Station to distant villages delivering goods that had arrived and collecting parcels and crates and huge packages ready for the next day's train. Old Tom drove the truck and all the traders knew him well. His daily round took quite a while as he stopped for a chat with the baker, had a drink at The Cobblers Arms and a cup of tea wherever it was offered.

The passenger trains along the line were great fun. A little Victorian locomotive with a shrill whistle pulled and pushed the local trains. Two carriages were coupled to it and the driver was in the locomotive one way but at the front of the first carriage for the return journey. As the train approached each station or halt there would be a shrill whistle from the locomotive and every passenger knew the train was coming. Regular travellers were well known to the guard and if someone was missing from the platform the train never went without them. Late running? What did that matter? A few minutes could soon be made up before Salchester was reached, more or less on time.

When even smaller stations were staffed, my grandmother told me there had been a porter at Chamford who would call out, 'Humbury, Dumbury, Martstone and Salchester!' as the train approached; thus offering his own appreciation of local place names. Even strangers soon realized that 'Dumbury' was his version of Deanbury.

*A little Victorian locomotive with a shrill whistle
pulled and pushed the local trains*

Faster trains used the line but never stopped at the rural stations. Some stopped at Humbury as such a busy little market town deserved a good service. One day an enterprising masked youth went to the booking office at Humbury and demanded the takings. He hadn't reckoned that Vicky Trotter would confront him. 'Don't be stupid!' she said and slammed an ebony ruler down on his fingers. The would-be thief roared with pain and fled through the station door into the bulk of P.C. Burman who was on his rounds and hoping for a cup of tea and a chat with Vicky.

Trains from other areas served Humbury Station. When I was waiting there on one occasion a gleaming green locomotive arrived. The chimney was topped with polished copper, the safety valve cover was sparkling brass and the whole locomotive oozed elegance and grace. Looking closely at this immaculate locomotive I saw the letters GWR on a plate that also told me that she was built in 1929. How different this was from the black machines that hauled most of the trains on the line. At that moment I fell in love with GWR engines of all shapes and sizes.

On an autumn day passengers waiting at the stations

didn't hear the shrill whistle of the local train. Instead there was a crisp 'toot toot' that seemed out of place. But 'toot toot' was there to stay. Diesel units had taken over the services. They were dull and characterless and had heavy thumping engines that resounded through the woods and valleys. The trains may have been cleaner, maybe a little faster, but they were no better. Passenger numbers increased, which was a good thing as the goods traffic was on the wane, road transport being quicker and more convenient.

When the harsh winter came, 'toot toot' fell silent. The weather was so very cold that the diesel fuel was frozen and there were no trains for a few days. One morning a shrill sound was heard as steam returned to the line. The little locomotive with its two push-pull carriages had not been scrapped, there hadn't been time, and so it was pressed back into service for several weeks until there was a thaw and the diesel units could be used again. Steam came to the rescue and the services were well patronized, as roads were treacherous. Many of the lanes in the area remained ice-bound for weeks. The slightest thaw would be followed by a severe frost, making them too dangerous for many people.

A few years passed and notices were posted announcing the closure of the line. Surveys had been completed that revealed that this section of the railway system was running at a loss. Naturally the surveys had been made during an autumn half term holiday when no children used the railway to go to school. A week sooner and many of the trains would have been packed. In the summer most trains were at least busy and just before Christmas each year hoards of shoppers used the line to go to Humbury, Boshampton and Salchester. There were meetings and proposals and protestations, all to no avail. The line was going to close. There was the suspicion that this had been decided months beforehand and nothing could prevent the closure.

On the last day of services the trains were full and the final train of the day was greeted at some stations by brass bands and crowds of railway mourners who couldn't accept that the end had come.

The little Victorian locomotive

Today the line is busier than ever as it has become a heritage railway. Sometimes a little Victorian locomotive puffs along the rails with two coaches, whistling before each station. Crowds come to see the historic locomotives, to enjoy the beauties of the line and to sniff the steam, so in the end steam has won and a piece of Forest charm has survived.

Ghosts In The Graveyard

Whytteford Church is situated down a long, quiet lane slightly away from the village. Walking that way is always a peaceful pleasure and on a warm summer's evening nowhere could be more delightful. The few fields by the lane give way to a woodland that can be a place for many delights. The trees, the softness and the secrecy of the woodland can capture you and draw you in. There are many hidden places well known and well used by courting couples for their pleasures as nowhere could be better for secluded summer loving.

The churchyard itself is always well tended. Harry Bannage was the verger for many years. He would often go to there late in the day when it was too hot to work in the full sun. You'd see his lanky figure cycle slowly to the church but for the last few hundred yards he'd coast down the hill gathering speed and enjoying the breeze. He'd tuck his bicycle beside the lych gate, unlock the little shed behind the church and get out his scythe.

'Why do you use a scythe, Harry?'

'Niver get one of they mowers raund the gravestonns.'

And he was right. A mower might reach some parts but the graves, the humps and lumps and molehills would make it quite impractical. So Harry would scythe away slicing the sharp blade through the grass and sliding the tip neatly into corners and between the memorials to the families of Whytteford.

Harry always took refreshment with him. Like my great-grandfather, Harry liked his ale so he took a couple of bottles to keep him satisfied and some thick sandwiches to keep him strong. On one hot day as the evening sun began to cast long shadows Harry finished his work and put the scythe away. He still had a sandwich left and half a bottle of beer so he sat himself against a gravestone and enjoyed his food, washing it down with the ale. He was wearing a light shirt with a neckerchief and pale moleskin trousers tied round the ankles to stop insects and wasps climbing to parts that Harry didn't want them to reach. On his head was a vast floppy straw hat to protect him from the heat.

The sun had been hot, the work had been long, the ale was relaxing and Harry was soon fast asleep against the gravestone. Gradually the sun faded from the sky but the night remained light, as this was high summer. A perfect day was coming to its close. The moon shone in the clear sky and bats began to fly over the church, round the trees and through the lych gate. Harry slept for over an hour and his hat slid to the ground.

Just after Harry fell asleep Daisy Midgely, escaping from her father's strict rule, met Mike Gilpin by the lych gate. They greeted each other with urgent delight and their plans for woodland loving were soon forgotten. Why walk so far when there was plenty of seclusion on the far side of the churchyard? They made their way through the tombstones and by the graves to the little gate behind the church. They slipped through and settled in a quiet spot behind a hedge where not even an owl or a bat would disturb their passion.

The lych gate

From the nearby woodland Joe Gramble and the shapely Bessie Maybury emerged. It being summer, Bessie had worn a skimpy blouse that revealed much of her lovely femininity and a short skirt, so Joe was making sure she didn't get a chill. Every few yards they'd stop for another passionate embrace, as neither of them wanted the evening's loving to end. When they reached the lych gate Bessie pulled Joe to her and kissed him again and then tugged him under the gateway. One thing led to another and they were longer there than they might have intended.

Meanwhile Harry slept on. His beer had worked upon him so he was sound asleep. He didn't snore but he made a histy whistling noise each time he breathed out. Breaking from yet another passionate embrace, the lovers drew breath and were about to kiss again when Bessie pulled away. Harry let out a long whistling hiss and then another.

'What's that?' asked Bessie, and although she had been well warmed by Joe she shivered.

There was another long histy breath.

'I don't like it, 'tis not natural,' said Bessie.

Harry suddenly woke. He yawned loudly and put his floppy straw hat on his head. The moon was shining right behind him as he stood up and his head appeared from behind the gravestone. With his big hat and gaunt figure silhouetted and silvered by the moon, Harry looked like a character from another age. The sight sent shivers through Bessie and even Joe was shaken.

'Wh…wh…what…is it?' asked Bessie.

'I don't know and I i'nt staying,' answered Joe, and grasping Bessie in his arms he pulled her away from the churchyard and off to The Cobblers Arms for some much needed beer.

But Bessie and Joe were not alone in seeing strange sights that night. Daisy and Mike were lingering with their loving as they enjoyed each other and the evening's warmth until they had to tear themselves apart and walk back through the churchyard. Both were in light summer clothes, the moon silvered them and the tree shadows made them vague. Harry, still not truly awake, rubbed his eyes and looked about. He saw two shadowy figures drifting behind gravestones. He had never been there so late. He looked again. The figures had gone. Then they were there again but silently disappeared. Harry stood swaying, grabbed a gravestone and grasped his way from one memorial to another across to the lych gate. He mounted his bicycle and pedalled to The Cobblers Arms faster than he had cycled in years. Clearly shaken, he strode in and demanded a double whisky, with no water, and then he told his tale.

The Ballet Comes To Salchester

There was a big advertisement in the Salchester Journal. For the first time in years the ballet was coming to the Empress Theatre; so called because it opened in the year that Queen Victoria, with Disraeli's contrivance, became Empress of India. At the beginning of the week 'Sleeping Beauty' was to be performed and there would be performances of 'Coppélia' on Friday and Saturday. This caused much excitement amongst many of the Whytteford ladies, of all ages, and groans of agony or even terror among some of the men. Miss Appleton, who ran a small private nursery school in Chamford, announced that she would be giving some evening sessions to tell people about the two ballets. After hearing about the special dances and clever effects that would be included, many of the ladies were all the more determined to go.

'I want you to take me to the ballet,' Bessie told Joe after she'd been to one of Miss Appleton's evenings. 'Let's go and see the ' The Sleeping Beauty' as it sounds so lovely.'

Joe loved Bessie dearly and he didn't want to lose her. She had a very exciting body and knew how to please him when they had the chance in the woods or out on the common hidden in the hollow of the tumulus.

'There's something wonderful in it,' said Bessie, 'called rose adagio.'

'Is there? I wunner what rose adagio is.'

'I'm not sure,' said Bessie, 'but it's lovely. And don't worry, I'll make sure you have a nice evening.'

This encouraged Joe to book some tickets.

Next night, in The Cobblers Arms, Joe was feeling happy about a night out with Bessie but thought he ought to put forward a manly profile.

'I've got to go to the ballate,' he declared.

'What ballate?'

'The Sleeping Beauty,' he replied. 'Bessie says it's lovely.'

'You'm lucky to have Bessie, so take care of her.'

'I will.' Joe's head nodded gently. 'She sayz ther'z rose adarrgio.'

'What's that, then?'

'Zounds like a type of fertallizar,' said a deep voice from a corner.

Joe, wearing a light jacket and black trousers, looked very smart when he collected Bessie on the evening of the ballet. When she opened the door to him he stood open-mouthed, as he had never seen her look more beautiful or more desirable. She was wearing a short silky dress that clung to her petite shapely body and revealed a lot of her enticing breasts. With her natural blonde hair and sparkling eyes Bessie would rouse many a man's attention that evening. She was subtly made up and her perfume did nothing to help Joe calm down. In her high-heeled sandals she clicked down the path and slipped into Joe's little sports car giving him enticing glimpses of little pieces of lace and joys to come.

'Bessie, you look 'mazing.' Suddenly the evening looked more than promising to Joe.

'You look smart too, Joseph.'

Joe felt a glow of happiness, as when Bessie used his full name he knew that she was especially pleased with him.

Late that night Joe's car rocked furiously in a quiet spot used by lovers. It was a warm forest evening and a romantic moon gave the woodland a gentle silver gleam. The lovely Bessie looked like an erotic nymph in a forest glade. She perched, with a cushion on the bonnet of the car, her dress discarded, and gave Joe the most passionate loving he had ever known.

'Will you take me to see 'Coppélia' on Friday?'

How could he refuse? Bessie had promised him 'a nice evening' and another one was irresistible.

'Course I will, 'slong as you wear that dress.'

'I so love you, Joseph.'

'And oi loves you, my Bessie.'

And then the passion began all over again.

The following night Joe was in The Cobblers Arms enjoying a refreshing beer after a hard day's work.

"Ow was the ballate?' someone asked.

'Foine,' said Joe. 'We had a lovely evening.' He'd never spoken a truer word.

'Were the girls pretty?'

'Pretty, but too skinny far me. None os 'em was as lovely as Bessie.'

'Your Bessie'd raise more than a smile in any man!'

'Unless 'e was dead o'course.'

'Well, what 'appened then, in that rosey adarrgio?'

'Ah, that waz special, this girl, whoiy, she danced on the tips of 'er toes.'

The Rose Adagio

'Gor! How she do thart?'

'Did she 'ave special boots on?'

'Naw, she 'ad dainy little shoes. Oi've niver saene anythin' loike it.'

'What's 'Sleeping Beauty' abawt thenn?'

'Ah,' said Joe, feeling on safer ground. ''Tis abawt a princess who fawls asleep 'cos of a little prick.'

'Arrh,' said a deep voice from the corner. 'Some women is loike thaat.'

'Bessie liked it awl sah much, she wants to go agen on Friday.'

'Whart they doing then?'

'I can't remember, but I think it begins with a C. Bessie seys 'tis abawt a doll.'

"Ow can youm 'ave a ballate 'bout a doll? Since when 'ave dolls been able to dance?'

Joe had been thinking hard, trying to remember the name of the other ballet. Suddenly Joe's face brightened up.

'She says it's called Cop something. Cop or Copper or…'

'You mean 'tas a policeman in it?'

'Don' saund a very good name ter me.'

'Cop…Cop…,' Joe was trying hard to think of the name.

'You'm sure you got the roight name?'

'Cop…Cop ..,' said Joe, wracking his brains. 'Ah, Oi've got it; 'tis called 'Copulator'.'

Goodbye Great-Aunt Edna

I had quite a collection of great-aunts all of whom had outlived their husbands. Great-Aunt Brenda was prehistoric, Great-Aunt Mabel was scatterbrained, Great-Aunt Bessie the funniest and Great-Aunt Veronica the most cantankerous. Auntie Madge tried to dominate every one. She would often declare, 'I am your blood aunt.' As a family we decided she always missed the 'y' from the word blood. Great-Aunt Bessie from then on always signed her letters; *'Lots of love, Blood Aunt Bessie.'* And then she would add, *'P.S. How's the blood-y aunt?'*

Great-Aunt Edna was my favourite ancient relative. She was sprightly, humorous and immensely kind. When she was forty-two she had married a wealthy man, many years her senior, and had a life of luxury as a result. Her proud husband bought her expensive fashionable clothes and took her on holidays to Switzerland. As she had no children Edna was always interested in her many nephews and nieces and their numerous offspring.

Having moved away from The Forest when she was quite young, Aunt Edna had lost her rustic tones and spoke with barely any accent.

'Edna 'ad electrocution lessons,' explained my grandfather. I was about to correct him when my mother gave me a very firm kick under the lunch table and I kept quiet.

In later years Great-Aunt Edna lived in Salchester and we often visited her. She'd sit in a wing chair by a small fire with her feet almost in the grate. At Christmas time she might invite us for tea, which would be served in her dining room that was never heated unless people were in there. There would be an ample spread that we ate as we shivered. My mother would drink cups of scalding tea to keep her warm.

There was only one thing that upset Great-Aunt Edna. She was punctilious in all that she did and expected the same of others. If you arranged to meet her for coffee in the Georgian Coffee Shop in Salchester it was safest to arrive five minutes early, as Edna would already be there checking her watch. On one occasion her solicitor kept her waiting seven minutes whilst he completed work with another client. This was not good enough for Edna. She regarded the delay as a personal insult and took her business elsewhere.

Late one November Edna was taken ill. The doctor visited and privately told us that she wouldn't live much longer. He arranged care for her in Salchester Hospital.

'Poor old lady,' he said. 'She won't go quickly.'

He was right. Great-Aunt Edna lived another three weeks, lucid until the end. She didn't actually organise the ward in the hospital but the nurses soon realised that she liked her tea at four o'clock, a little supper at six o'clock and a hot drink at nine o'clock. One day, at exactly eleven o'clock in the morning, Edna breathed her last. We contacted some undertakers in Salchester to arrange her funeral.

Edna wanted to return to the village of her childhood and be buried with her relations in Whytteford churchyard. Unfortunately an icy frost had smothered The Forest for many days before Edna died and the ground was hard as rock. The soil was so solid that old Harry, the Verger, couldn't prepare the grave and so poor Great-Aunt Edna had a prolonged rest elsewhere.

Eventually the weather changed, the ground thawed, Harry could dig the grave and the funeral was arranged for a Friday just before Christmas. First Harry scythed the grass and then the digging began. He did the job very carefully, making sure there was a perfect rectangle for the coffin. He had a short ladder that he used when the hole became deep. Late on Thursday afternoon Harry had almost completed the digging of Edna's grave. It being a cloudy December day, by four o'clock the dusk was descending, the gloom being emphasised by the dark yew trees near the lych gate and along the paths of the churchyard. Harry kept on working.

Daisy Midgley and her boyfriend Micky Gilpin had few chances for loving as Daisy's father was very strict with her and gave firm instructions.

'You're cooking tonight. Get the meat in by six!' he'd said and Daisy dared not disobey. Provided she seemingly followed her father's rules she could get away with many things. That evening, as she walked homewards past the church, she looked towards the lych gate. Sure enough Micky was waiting for her and it was only five o'clock. They could have nearly an hour's passion and her father would be none the wiser. They slipped through the gate into a secluded corner of the graveyard, Micky spread out his big coat and the loving commenced.

Daisy was so passionate and Micky so loving that the exercise warmed them and they were not aware of Harry working away down in the grave. Suddenly Daisy sniggered.

'Something funny?' whispered Micky.

'Something Dad said.'

'What was that?'

'Get the meat in by six.'

'Then you must do as you're told and get the meat in!'

'I always do as I'm told,' she giggled. The passion continued and Daisy made sure she had obeyed her father.

As it was now virtually dark Harry had lit a lantern and slung it on a pole across the grave. He finished his work and began to climb from the hole. Harry was tired from his exertions and as he climbed he wheezed and panted noisily.

'What's…what's…what's that?' asked Daisy. Shivers ran through her that would not stop.

The lovers peered between the gravestones as Harry, his groans becoming louder, heaved himself from the grave with the lantern light shining from beneath him and emphasising his gaunt figure. A little mist was also rising from the damp ground, drifting around the grave and glowing in the soft lantern light.

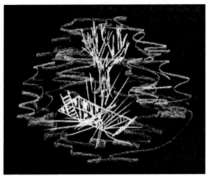

Lantern light shining from the grave

'I...don't...I don't...know...' Micky was shaking too as he saw this seemingly supernatural figure.

When he was out of the grave old Harry put on his big hat, swung his old coat over his back, lifted up the scythe onto his shoulder, and raised the lantern. Using his spade for support, he slowly plodded, grunted, whistled eerily and tunelessly through his teeth, and made his way towards the lovers who were close to the lych gate. Seeing this black-cloaked figure holding a scythe and lantern walking towards her, Daisy gasped in terror.

'He's coming for us!' she whimpered. Micky pulled her with all his strength out of the churchyard, along the lane and safely near to the lights of her home. Later, still nervous, he cautiously crept back to collect his coat.

Next day was Great-Aunt Edna's funeral. The undertakers, coming from Salchester, didn't know the area. My father and I, wearing thick overcoats, waited outside Whytteford Church, talking with the jovial Reverend Paston. He was wrapped in a warm black cloak. 'I was told to buy a cloak when I was ordained,' he explained. 'And I am very glad of it on days like this.'

Eventually the hearse arrived, over twenty minutes late.

'Sorry to be late. We couldn't find the church as we don't really know this area. We didn't realise it was so far from the rest of the village.'

The service could begin at last. Afterwards dear Great-Aunt Edna was lowered into her grave in the churchyard of the village she had known for over eighty years.

I must admit I smiled inwardly. Great-Aunt Edna would have been *so* embarrassed. Punctilious all her life she had kept people waiting by being late for her own funeral.

The Wedding

Bessie and Joe were to be married. This was scarcely sensational news as they had been enjoying a passionate romance for quite a few years. Joe was the envy of many young men as they all admired Bessie's shapely body and her enticing sexuality. To see Bessie in a fitting dress was an experience to be savoured. Seeing her on a hot day in summer was another delight that could not be forgotten.

The wedding was fixed for the middle of June and the preparations began.

'I'd like the whole village to be invited,' declared Bessie, 'but I know that would cost too much.'

'That depends on where you have the celebration,' said her mother. 'We could have it the old barn and lots of folks could join us.'

'We'll decorate the old beams with summer flowers and it will look magical,' Bessie said, her eyes gleaming in delight.

The barn was cleared of the accumulations from many years of hoarding. Defunct mowers were rediscovered, ancient tools turfed out of corners and loads of items that 'might be useful one day' were disturbed from years of rest. Trestle tables were scrubbed and chairs and benches borrowed. The day before the wedding gardens and hedgerows were raided for flowers. White blossoms, pink pastels and creamy woodbine were gathered from round the village and the barn was decorated. The fragrance added to the sweet fresh air of The Forest.

When the wedding day came rain was pouring down early in the morning. Bessie was in despair.

'Stop worrying,' said her mother. 'Rain before seven, fine before eleven! It's an old saying but it's often true.'

By eleven o'clock the clouds were being burnt off by the summer sun and The Forest was looking freshly painted in a multitude of natural shades. The hedgerows and verges along the lane to the church had not been cut and so pink, blue, white and cream wild flowers lined the route. Bessie and her father rode in a little open trap decorated with flowers and ribbons. The pony pulling it had tiny bouquets on its bridle.

In the church the villagers gathered. Everyone loved Bessie and Joe and so the old balcony had to be pressed into service for the first time since the funeral of the Master of the Hunt. Swathes of flowers and greenery made the little church look especially pretty and light as the sun sparkled through the coloured glass in the windows.

Joe waited patiently with his best man; he was longing to see what Bessie was wearing. Eventually Mrs Sponder managed to squeeze something approximating to 'Here comes the bride' from the harmonium and the whole congregation turned in their pews to see Bessie as she entered the little church with her father. Joe stared open mouthed. He saw a beautiful, shapely nymph in a white dress smiling as she came towards him. Her sparkling eyes and joyful smile added to the enchantment. Bessie was wearing a strapless dress that hugged her figure tightly at the top and as she breathed her beauty took on a special magnetism. The skirt of the dress hung from her waist and spread from her hips so that instead of walking Bessie almost seemed to glide down the aisle. Joe felt so proud of his Bessie that he had a lump in his throat.

A shapely nymph in a creamy white dress

The singing was rousing throughout the service and when it was Joe's turn to say 'I do!' everyone knew that he meant it. And Bessie was equally clear when she spoke. When the Reverend Phillip Paston at last said, 'You may kiss the bride,' Joe kissed well and Bessie was reluctant to break the kiss, as she was so happy. The service over, everyone crowded into photographs. The photographer stood on top of the churchyard wall for some of the pictures and despite a few precarious moments, that caused much hilarity, he somehow managed to include everyone in some of the pictures.

Bessie and Joe walked out through the lych gate and then Joe lifted Bessie into the little trap. Naturally the photographer recorded that scene as well. And then they drove off showered in rose petals thrown by the wedding guests. Bessie sat close to Joe as he held the reins and the pony, almost left to find its own way, set off up the hill and along the lane.

As they passed through some woodland Bessie suddenly took the reins.

'Where are we going?' asked Joe as Bessie steered off the road into a little glade.

'Just a little diversion,' murmured Bessie. She pulled on the reins and the pony came to a halt. 'Time for a proper kiss.'

Bessie pulled Joe to her and they kissed with gusto, as there was no audience. The pony put its head down and tasted fresh grass and the kiss went on accompanied by the sound of munching and snorting. Reluctantly the newly married lovers pulled themselves apart.

'We'd better move on,' said Joe. He took the reins and flicked them, the pony moved off and he flicked them again so that it trotted smartly to Bessie's home and pulled up outside the barn.

'Where have you been?' chorused the guests, most of whom had already arrived from the church.

'Pony needed a rest on the way,' said Joe but nobody believed him. Instead there were guffaws of laughter. Bessie laughed as well and let her sparkling eyes tell their own tale.

The summer sun now shone from a cloudless sky. The great barn doors were opened wide and the festivities of the happiest wedding in The Forest for many years began. At many weddings family feuds surface, there are arguments and sometimes fights break out, but this day was too splendid and too joyous for such things. On a long table was a feast of freshly baked rolls, cheeses and meats. A pig had been roasted over a spit outside the barn and delicious smells wafted round the garden and into the barn. Gradually an evening glow came over the scene as the sun slowly set. Lanterns were hung from the beams and the festivities went on into the night.

What could have been happier? Could any occasion have been more joyous than Bessie and Joe's wedding in The Forest?

Drama And Melodrama

Nobody admitted to having had the idea but news of it spread very quickly and, before anyone realised what they had let themselves in for, it was going to happen. The villagers of Whytteford were going to put on a Christmas show. 'Babes in the Wood' was chosen and unsuspecting villagers, who had never admitted to any thespian skills, were persuaded to take part. Almost everyone, other than the very elderly and the very young, had something to do. Who was the organising and motivating force behind this grand scheme? It was the multi-talented Jeb Carpenter; although he insisted or pretended that the idea had been thought of by someone else. But once Jeb made up his mind to do something then it was going to happen.

He visited everybody in the village and would have a gentle chat before mentioning 'Babes in the Wood' and slipping in a seemingly slight request. Not giving time for anyone to refuse Jeb said, 'That's really kind. Thank you.' And before there was a chance to say anything more he was gone.

Old Henry was approached whilst he was working in his garden. Henry suddenly concentrated on his beans and tried not to look up. He had a habit of suddenly suffering from deafness but he was no match for Jeb.

'Fine crop you'm gart there, Henry!' Jeb fog-horned across the garden and even Henry could not pretend he hadn't heard. 'I need some advice about beetroot,' he added and within moments Henry was engaged in a deep conversation about gardening. In a few minutes Jeb was gone and Henry suddenly realised that he had agreed to join in 'Babes in the Wood'; playing the part of the Ghost. When he next saw Jeb in The Cobblers Arms he tried to remonstrate but to no avail.

'You'll love it, t'is easy. All you'm 'ave t'do is go 'Whooo!' and 'Ahhh!' an you'm be fine.'

'He does thart most of the toime,' someone was heard to

mutter.

'Jus' act normal, Henry,' said Joe, who was looking forward to being Robin Hood.

'Ahhh,' said Henry. 'Whooo, s'pose I can do it.'

'Toype carstin' if you'm arsk me,' rumbled a deep voice in the corner.

'Let's 'ave a drink, then,' said Jeb. Henry was won over, as he never refused a drink if someone else was buying.

"Ow will I know when to speeeake?'

'I'll prompt yer.'

'Foine. Oi'll do it.'

The choice of 'Babes in the Wood' was ideal as it meant that plenty of children could be involved as well as the two playing the Babes. Bessie was chosen to play Maid Marion and she was delighted, even offering to make her own costumes. The prospect of the show led to much discussion. Who would be the evil Sheriff of Nottingham? Who would be Friar Tuck? Little John? Nurse Mollycoddle? Will Scarlet? Then there were the two thugs, Hammer and Chisel; who would fill those roles?

Many wanted the rehearsals to be held in the big back room at The Cobblers but Jeb insisted that rehearsals would be in the Village Hall, which was conveniently close to the hostelry for the moment when each rehearsal finished. 'We'll not go on late,' promised Jeb. 'There'll be plenty of toime for drinks arfter. And don' you'm go bringing beer to the rehoirsals,' he added firmly. The rehearsals were good fun, especially once some attempt had been made to learn lines.

The main problem after a few weeks was that the cast knew their words quite well but many were never sure when they should speak them. Old Henry made much melodrama of 'Whooo!' and his 'Ahhh!' could make the windows rattle but he had no idea when his spectacular talents were needed. Jeb tried to impress on Henry that he only appeared towards the end of show during the scene in Nottingham Castle.

Ella Landy was Wardrobe Mistress. She coaxed and cajoled anybody that she knew and suitable clothes that could be adjusted and adapted appeared from the backs of wardrobes, from jumble sales and market stalls. Jeb used his artistic talents and produced sets that would have graced any theatre. His woodland scenes were a total delight. Those who knew The Forest well even realised that they were based on real places.

Jeb produced sets that would have graced any theatre

'Joe,' said Bessie, as she surveyed a moonlit scene, 'isn't that where we went after the ballet?'

'Hush,' whispered Joe, 'though I reckon you'm roight!' A flash of delight passed between them. 'Happy mem'ries, Bessie,' he added. 'We must go there again.' She gave him a wonderfully provocative smile that meant that for the rest of the rehearsal Joe was unable to deliver a single line correctly.

Dress rehearsals are not meant to go well. The final rehearsal of 'Babes in the Wood' went very well and everyone went to their homes or The Cobblers happy and confident. That was when the trouble began. The cast was too confident and so they relaxed and pre-show nerves were almost non-existent. The first performance was for people from homes for the elderly from Humbury and surrounding villages. Jeb had forgotten to warn the cast not to drink before the performance and many visited The Cobblers for a 'quick one'.

At twenty past seven the little hall was full. The old folks had been brought out, wrapped in scarves, shawls and rugs, as it was a cold night. From the tightly packed audience the scents of mothballs and embrocation emanated and as the lighting heated up the hall the smells permeated every corner. Meanwhile Jeb sent an urgent message to The Cobblers and the cast hastily finished their drinks then belted along the road to the back of the hall. Some were already in costume but others scrambled into what they thought looked right and the performance began. As he wasn't needed for a long time old Henry settled himself in a corner and fell asleep.

Muddled lines and confused costumes left the audience baffled. Why was Robin Hood in red and Will Scarlet in green? Maid Marian looked fine and many old male eyes admired the way the costume hugged Bessie, especially whenever she bent forward.

'Wahey!' cried one old boy. 'Wahey!'

His enthusiastic call awoke Henry who sprung from his corner and, thinking he'd been prompted, launched himself into the woodland glade.

'Whooo! Whooo!'

Alarmed by this unexpected outburst Bessie spun round, catching her foot in her dress. A ripping sound was heard and she revealed more than she had ever intended.

'Wahey! Wahey!' cried the old boy in the audience.

'Ahhh! Ahhh! Whooo! Whooo!' boomed the Ghost as

played by Henry.

This was the cue for smoke to fill the stage during the siege of Nottingham Castle. Mistaking Henry's cry, young Morris Bunden, who was in charge of the effects, pressed the trigger on the smoke machine. A huge white puff billowed from the wings filling the woodland glade and also helping Bessie to regain some modesty. Jeb made a wise decision and closed the curtains. The audience thought it was time for the interval and clapped enthusiastically, mistaking the white smoke for woodland mist and thinking the effect was wonderful.

During the interval a blushing Bessie was seen frantically doing some needlework on her dress and Jeb called the cast together for some stern words. Costumes were reassigned to characters and everyone prepared for Act Two. This also had to include the final scene of the curtailed Act One and so the stage was set for Robin Hood's secret headquarters.

Jeb filled the role of Friar Tuck superbly

Jeb filled the role of Friar Tuck superbly. Even his substantial figure had to be padded out for this part. He kept a flask at his side, hidden in his robes, so that he could

119

take a swig from time to time.

'What's in there?' asked Joe.

'Just something to keep my throat fresh,' said Jeb as he rammed the cork in tightly and let the flask get hidden amongst his robes again. Scenes that Jeb was in went well as he had learnt his lines perfectly. He actually knew the entire script and gave subtle prompts when needed. When Jeb was offstage the prompts still came. They tended to be rather too loud but the elderly audience remained oblivious.

Jeb kept Old Henry firmly in his chair at the side of the stage. But Henry was not asleep all of the time. Suddenly he noticed Jeb's flask swaying just in front of his face. As it swung he grabbed it and quickly pulled out the cork, sniffed the fumes of whisky and put the flask to his lips. Jeb, who was perfectly still as the scene on stage was going well, failed to realise what was happening. Henry drank deeply and then settled into his corner with a smile on his face.

The school scene with Nurse Mollycoddle swept along. The children knew their words and songs and the elderly audience were enchanted. The school scene ended and the children laughed and chattered as they carried off benches and Nurse Mollycoddle led an audience participation number. The old folks did their best to keep up with 'Knees up Mother Brown' but as it was played faster and faster they finished three bars behind the pianist.

Hammer and Chisel, the Sheriff's rogues acted dumbly in a scene at the front of the stage The Sheriff gave them orders and they responded with ancient jokes that had the old folks howling with laughter.

'Find me a fine horse!' said the Sheriff standing close to Hammer.

'Right-oh!'

'And I'll need a helmet.'

'Right-oh!'

'I'll need a sharp sword.'

'Right-oh!'

'Why do keep saying right-oh?'

'Because you're standing on it.'

'What am I standing on?'

'My right toe!'

'How do you manage to do so many stupid things every day?'

'I get up very early.'

Hammer and Chisel were enjoying themselves and the audience was laughing. The script was semi-discarded as joke after joke tumbled from their lips. In the wings Jeb was trying to signal that the scene must end. Eventually he reached out with a long walking stick and pulled Hammer. Where-ever Hammer went Chisel followed. The Sheriff fortunately remembered the scene's final line. 'Bring me Robin Hood, dead or alive,' he bellowed, 'or you'll be locked in a tool chest and I'll throw the key into the moat!' Then he strode off stage.

During that extended scene the stage had been set for the siege of Nottingham Castle. This was to be the spectacular climax of the evening. The battlements were solid and a flag fluttered, gently pulled by thin nylon strings.

There was a mighty boom as cannon fired and the old folks were shaken in their seats and they frantically clung on to their sticks and walking frames. And then the siege began.

'Robin Hood! You are doomed!' the Sheriff roared.

A torrent of polystyrene rocks was hurled over the castle battlements.

'You'll never, never capture me!'

The tops of scaling ladders appeared on the walls and Robin Hood and his Merry Men began to appear. Suddenly, from a doorway in the castle, the Ghost appeared. 'Whooo! Whooo!' The audience laughed loudly! 'Ahhh! Ahhh! Whooo! Whooo!' Then he disappeared and settled down in the corner, and being a ghost full of strong spirit, he fell fast asleep.

This was the signal for another cannon explosion and a great cloud of smoke. The walls shuddered and gave way to reveal the full force of the outlaws.

'Hold back!' roared the Sheriff. 'I have someone you will not want to kill!' Hammer and Chisel dragged in Maid Marian and held her for Robin Hood to see.

'Wahey!' shouted the excitable old man, his eyes focussed on Bessie. 'Wahey!'

'Be quiet, Trevor!'

'Wahey!'

The action seemed to have shifted from the stage to the audience but Trevor was somehow subdued and the show went on.

'Robin! Robin! Look out!' Marian cried as the Sheriff took hold of her and pushed Hammer and Chisel towards him.

But Robin and Little John grabbed the incompetent rogues' swords and then pinned the Sheriff to the castle wall and Maid Marian was freed!

Suddenly there was a great cheer as King Richard I strode on, home from the Crusades. And so there was a grand happy ending with Maid Marian marrying Robin Hood in the presence of the King.

At the curtain call Bessie, tantalising as ever in her figure-hugging costume, gave a deep curtsey.

'Wahey! Wahey!' cried the suddenly revived Trevor.

The Ghost, woken from his slumbers by all the noise, strode on stage again. 'Whooo! Whooo!' he bellowed.

'Wahey! Wahey!' cried Trevor as the cast bowed once more.

'Whooo! Ahhh! Ahhh! Whooo!' the Ghost responded shaking his fists. Mistaking this for another cue Morris Bunden fired the smoke machine again and the cast were enveloped in a white cloud as the curtains closed on a truly memorable evening.

Santa Claus's Happy Christmas

'Could you come and be Santa Claus at the Christmas Party?' asked the jovial Reverend Paston, Rector of Whytteford church.

This was quite a surprise. I had returned to the village for the festive season and I was looking forward to a traditional Christmas. I had not anticipated this request.

'The party is in the hall tomorrow,' said the jolly rector. 'You see,' he explained, 'the children don't know you and so you'd be ideal.'

'I think I might be a bit young,' I said.

'That's not a problem. We have a very good costume and Jack will help you with some make up. You'll be very well disguised. Please do it. Jeb's not too well and really isn't up to it.'

To my amazement I found myself agreeing to act as Santa Claus for a party of children I didn't know. Apparently there would be a nativity play, and then Santa Claus would arrive and be full of festive cheer. He would give out presents and afterwards there would be tea and games for the children whilst their parents quaffed mulled wine, devoured cheeses and mince pies before struggling home with their over-excited offspring.

'Come along about 3.30,' said the rector, 'then they won't see you arrive.'

'Fine...er...er...who's Jack?' But the rector had gone before I could finish the sentence.

And so I arrived at the back door of the village hall at 3.30pm the next day, clutching some black Wellington boots, hoping that the approaching ordeal would soon be over.

'There you are,' said a bright voice the moment I opened the door. 'I'm Jack.' I stood open mouthed. There in front of me was a smiling bright-eyed young lady of my own age. Suddenly this dull December afternoon seemed much better. I wouldn't say my nerves evaporated but they certainly were no longer so dominant in my mind. I admired her shapely figure, emphasized by the tight top she was wearing, admired the long legs revealed by her short skirt and enjoyed thoughts not usually associated with Santa Claus.

'Come on, you'd better get changed. Here's the costume.'

I popped in to the gentleman's lavatory and some minutes later emerged in scarlet robes with a black belt and black boots.

'Well done…but I think you look a bit slim. I guess Jeb Carpenter must be bigger than you. Let's try this.' She produced a cushion that she stuffed under my costume, hands moving nimbly as she adjusting everything so that I looked 'natural' and not padded.

'Thank you,' I gasped. 'What now?'

'Time for the make up.'

This was a new experience. I had never been made up before and having it done by a delectable young lady, standing very close, smiling and enveloping me in her exotic perfume, meant that the experience was entirely pleasurable. After the make up some whiskers were added and a beard.

'There, it's all done. Look in the mirror.'

I looked and saw an old man staring back at me. The only features I recognized were my nose and my eyes.

'That's wonderful. Nobody will recognize me.'

'Now put on a deep voice, and give lots of "Ho! Ho! Hoes" and you'll be fine. All the packets in the sack are named.' She thrust a heavy hessian sack into my gloved hands.'

The nativity play was coming to its conclusion. It would soon be time for my grand entrance.

'When each child comes up they can sit on your knee so that the mums and dads can take photographs.'

I didn't relish this idea but I had to go along with it.

'By the way, Miss Appleton says don't let the little girl playing Mary sit on your knee. She can be a bit damp at times.'

The final carol of the play ended. There was some applause and then an outburst of chatter. Jack started to ring some sleigh bells very loudly and when she stopped I hammered on the door. Suddenly there was silence and a voice said, 'I wonder who that can be.' I hammered on the door again and it was opened. 'Jingle Bells' was played and sung in various keys and I strode in to the room. There was a gasp from the tiny children and I boomed, 'Merry Christmas!' Everyone clapped and I began to feel more at ease. To my own amazement I told stories about elves working to make presents, about loading my sleigh and flying through the sky. I explained why I had to be careful as I steered my reindeer and that they had to have a rest from time to time. The children sat open mouthed seemingly believing my tale.

'Don't let the little girl playing Mary sit on your knee. She can be a bit damp at times.'

The rest of my time as Santa Claus went amazingly well. I called out the names on the parcels and the youngsters came up to me. Some were shy, some were chatty and all of them had their photographs taken. Looking up I could see Jack standing at the back, smiling encouragement. It was easy to spot Mary in her nativity costume. She stood next to me to receive her gift, her picture was taken and I remained dry. My job was done. 'A Merry Christmas to you all!' I exclaimed and to the sound of cheers and bells I waved farewell.

Jack greeted me with a huge smile and laughing eyes. 'You were great. That was such fun.' She gave me an appreciative kiss. 'Now let's get you changed and we can go for a drink.'

What could have been more delightful? Out of my disguise I was happy to get to know Jack much better.

'Why are you Jack?'

'You'd change your name if you'd be christened Jacinta. My parents could have been more thoughtful.'

'And what brings you to The Forest at Christmas?'

'I'm staying with Uncle Philip and Auntie May.'

'I'm glad I've met you.'

'It's lovely to meet you.' And she lent over and gave me a memorable kiss. 'Could you take me out this evening?' Her eyes gleamed and sparkled.

'Well, Santa will have to ask you a question.'

'What's that?'

'Are you a good girl?'

'Perhaps you'll find out later.' And she began to giggle. Laughter is so infectious; I began to laugh too.

'Of course I'll take you out.'

'And I promise I'll be good.'

Wattle And Daub

Whytteford Church is some way from the rest of the village; situated by the tiny but gushing River Coble it nestles among trees in the valley. In the summer it is a blissful place but in the winter this can be the coldest part of the village. Not far away is Manor Farm but other homes are few and well away from the place of worship.

When I was young the separation of church and village puzzled me but, as Jeb Carpenter explained, there was a simple answer. Whytteford is an old village and at one time there had been a cluster of rustic dwellings near the church. The Black Death came but failed to wipe out the population. Those that survived decided that they would have to move away from the damp area near the church, as it wasn't healthy. And so the centre of the village moved to higher and drier land, only half a mile away and still within the parish. This may seem like a major upheaval but the construction of a house didn't take long.

Wattle and daub were the traditional building materials and a home could be created within quite a short time. Beech stakes were driven into the earth and the split hazel lathes and heather were woven between them. A mixture of wet soil, clay, sand and animal dung was applied, creating a thick wall that took a while to dry out. Timber supports held the roof that was then thatched with reeds. Gradually the structures became more sophisticated. Many homes had a rudimentary cruck frame and bricks were used to create an open fireplace with a chimney up through the whole structure and that kept the home warm. If cracks appeared in the walls nobody was worried. They were soon filled up with more sticky daub. Often decoration had been scraped into the top surface. One cottage had a most artistic floral design.

The ground floor was of beaten earth looking like golden concrete that had been polished by use. Sometimes in a dry summer the floors might develop cracks but nobody seemed to worry about them. Often the once level floors tilted to one side or dipped in the middle. My grandfather told me about Auntie Brenda's cottage. Brenda had decided that she wanted a proper floor. Mistaking the beaten earth for concrete, my grandfather had broken it up with a pickaxe, cleared it away and attempted to find the foundations of the cottage. He could have dug forever, as these cottages never had any foundations. Curiously the shed in which the ancient Brenda kept her cow was made of bricks, so the cow had better quality accommodation than the people.

Out on the common there was a rather attractive pool that always had water in it. Dug out of the clay soil it never went dry however long the area went without rain. Nearby were many of the older cottages of the village including one where Jeb Carpenter, captain of the village cricket team, lived with his lively family. To me the pool, which was busy with wildlife, didn't seem quite natural. 'Caws it n'int natral,' he explained, 'orl the clay for the cattages wuz dug frum thar.'

Many of these cottages have gradually been replaced but a lot still exist and are now regarded as historic and characterful. The attractive thatch and irregular shapes, no two cottages being alike, give The Forest villages distinct personality. Although modern developments such as mains water and electricity came to Whytteford over sixty years ago they didn't change the ways of some villagers. Several cottages still have wells that provide good, cool fresh water on the hottest of days and not long ago one cottage had electricity downstairs but the owner had never seen the need to have it upstairs. Damp courses have been added and brick-built bathrooms have been tacked on, usually in a characterless way.

Mrs Landy lived in a wattle and daub cottage of indeterminate age. Tucked away in a quiet spot the cottage was cosy in the winter as she always had a blazing fire; in the summer it was pleasantly cool and there were good views from the little windows although some of the glass was so ancient that your vision would be distorted. One room had been separated to create a tiny kitchen and bathroom. Upstairs there were two bedrooms. The floors sloped at peculiar angles, the beds needed extra support on some corners, but the rooms were a delight. Admittedly it was dangerous to get out of bed too energetically and risk banging your head on a beam. There could be this unexpected bounce, as the floors in these cottages seemed to have an unusual quality, probably because everything used in the building was very flexible.

A wattle and daub cottage of indeterminate age

But Mrs Landy was not content. New homes for the elderly were being created and she wanted to live in one. As she was over seventy and living in such a crude dwelling she was soon allocated a new flat. A few months after she moved Mrs Landy was clearly unhappy. She didn't like the modern home. The neighbourhood was busy, the flat was dull, she could hear her neighbours, the rooms were too light... Mrs Landy was missing her cottage. She couldn't go back to it as without an inhabitant the cottage had lost interest in life. Wet weather meant that it had started to weaken as no fires had been lit to keep it dry. Strong wind had torn the thatch and in less than a year the cottage was falling apart. One night a strong wind blew heavy rain on to one of the walls and it began to crumble and then fell.

For Mrs Landy this was the end of all hope. She couldn't even dream of returning to her cottage and so she passed away. The remains of the cottage gradually became overgrown, trees grew where once there had been a snug room and as time passed the cottage once more became part of nature. Mrs Landy didn't want to live without her cottage and the cottage could not live without Mrs Landy.

Elsie And Lionel

Elsie and Lionel were an elderly couple who didn't seem to realize that they were becoming older. They lived life at a hectic pace that was an example to many people fifty years younger. When he was in his eighties Lionel still put on waders and went fishing deep in the rivers and Elsie would go on walks with younger people who couldn't keep up with her. Whenever I returned to Whytteford I always paid them a visit.

'Come and see us,' Elsie would say. 'Come for coffee on Saturday.'

'Have a gin and tonic. It's far quicker and much less work. Less washing up too.'

I was never given any coffee. As soon as I arrived sherry, gin and whisky were always offered.

'I thought I had come for coffee.'

'Have a gin and tonic. It's far quicker and much less work. Less washing up too.' I didn't like to argue with this interesting attitude.

When he was nearly ninety Lionel was still driving and he was certainly in full control. He didn't like country lanes as there were too many twists and turns. Because of this he seldom went in to Humbury, preferring the faster main road to Salchester. Travelling far and wide he often completed a

131

journey of over one hundred and fifty miles in less than two and a half hours.

'I did try to keep under ninety miles an hour,' he once said.

'What about the police?' I asked.

'They're too slow to catch me,' he said with a twinkle.

'And if they did catch him they'd think their cameras were wrong,' added Elsie, 'as no-one of his age would ever drive at that speed.'

At one time there was a scare about the safety of eating beef. There was a fear that the human brain might be affected and madness might follow.

'We're not bothered by this beef business,' said Elsie. 'Why should we at our age?'

'Do you think anyone would notice?' I said. It just slipped out of my mouth. I thought I had gone too far as I was given a stern look. A moment later Elsie was laughing loudly.

'That's good,' she said. 'That's one to remember.'

'He's right too,' chuckled Lionel.

One evening when I visited, and we were half way through the first gin and tonics, there was a knocking at their door. This was proper loud knocking as there was nothing timid about it. Neither of them moved.

'That's just George. He always knocks about this time.'

'George? Who is George?'

'We've never seen him. We've been to the door many a time but there's never anyone there.'

'Sometimes we smell pipe tobacco. That's George as well.'

'What do you mean?'

'When we first moved here we heard the knocking and we thought we could smell the tobacco so we decided George was responsible.'

'Why did you call him George?'

'First name we thought of.'

'And the funny thing is someone called George did live

here about a century ago.'

'That's right. He was a gardener at Challington Manor.'

'So you see, we were right. It was George who knocked at the door and smoked a pipe.'

When Elsie was eighty-six and Lionel ninety-two I visited them one Monday evening. We drank gin and chatted and laughed.

Just as I was leaving Elsie asked, 'What are you doing tomorrow?'

'I was thinking of going into Salchester.'

'On a Tuesday?' She sounded shocked. 'We *never* go to Salchester on a Tuesday. It's pension day. There are too many old people about and they get in the way!'

In The Solicitors' Office

Tucked away in a side street of Humbury were Harnett and Oggins, Solicitors and Commissioners for Oaths. Their premises dated from the Georgian era and throughout the chambers there was a distinct atmosphere of another age. Pile upon pile of legal papers and files filled the offices. How the legal gentlemen struggled between them, but somehow they tottered about, disturbing nothing except dust. Each desk too was piled with current or fairly current work. You sat opposite the legal gentleman who was attending to your problems or requirements. He would peer between heaps of legality then bob behind them to check a fact, figure or precedent; then he would survey you again.

Reginald Quintus Harnett had founded the firm in the year of Queen Victoria's Diamond Jubilee and his son, Clarence, joined him in the reign of George V. He lead the legal team well into the reign of the young Elizabeth II, wearing a morning coat, dark grey striped trousers and a wing-collared shirt throughout every legal day. Daniel Montmorency Oggins joined the firm in the reign of George VI and continued working every day on legal minutiae until he was nearly eighty. He then became a part-time partner outliving most of the clients for whom he had prepared wills. He too dressed formally with starched collar and gleaming spotted bow tie.

You entered the office by climbing six steps, then through a doorway framed by classical columns. A solid black Georgian door led to what might today be called 'reception' but here amounted to Miss Twindle sitting tweedily behind a massive desk. The ceiling was high and lined with solid, strong oak shelves full of legal books and legal files providing history and instance should it ever be needed. A thin layer of dust before each volume suggested that most of these aids to law were seldom consulted. Thin lines of unbroken cobwebs tended to confirm these suspicions. You could hear what might be the sound of a typewriter but it could also be Miss Twindle's knitting needles clacking away as she made progress on yet another garment for nieces and nephews. She would look up but the clacking sound would continue.

'Go on up,' she would say and clients were left to find their own route up the twisty stairs to either Mr Oggins or the latest Mr Harnett.

An important and potentially long appointment with Oggins was memorable as when he looked at you across his desk he would lean forward and stare with gleaming black eyes that seemed to be searching your thoughts and penetrating your mind. Suddenly he would swivel on his ancient office chair, open a cupboard and produce bottles and glasses.

'This will take a little while; we need sustenance. Gin or whisky?' he always spoke slightly ponderously giving special emphasis to some words.

'A weak gin would be nice.'

'What's the point of weak when you've not far to go?

'But I'll be driving.'

'Since when have you seen the police on the roads between here and Whytteford? If they stop you I'll soon sort them out!' Then he would bellow down the stairs. 'A few cubes of ice please, Miss Twindle. Quite a few, if you would be so kind.'

Whilst he and a client consumed gin or whisky Oggins would genially ponder and pronounce his views about farming, hunting, the local agricultural show or any current local topic that had been featured in the Humbury Advertiser. Sustenance consumed, he reverted to business with eagle eyes and sharpened brain.

In this delightfully archaic world conveyancing was completed, wills were made and subsequently read and discussed. Spirits were raised and dreams demolished, tears were shed and surprises, not all welcome, relayed in legal terminology to the delight, despondency, dismay and bemusement of clients. The offices of solicitors can be dispiriting places; the unchanging world of Harnett and Oggins being no exception. If Reginald Quintus Harnett had strolled into the offices of the practice he had founded he would have recognised almost everything, even the original typewriter, purchased in 1897, was still there in case its modern replacement, purchased decades later, should fail. He would have noticed that there were more legal tomes and records but these were in addition to all the ones that he had known, not replacements for them. Even the telephone was archaic but not old enough for Harnett to have used it.

The original typewriter, purchased in 1897, was still there

My elderly friend Lionel had to visit Harnett and Oggins to swear an affidavit. All was ready, exhibits had been verified and the affidavit was due to be sworn.

'Now,' said Mr Oggins thrusting a book into Lionel's hand, 'hold this Bible in your hand and say these words.' Lionel held the book high and Oggins held up a card for him to read.

'I swear by Almighty God that this is my name and handwriting and that the contents of this, my affidavit, are true,' boomed Lionel and he passed the book back to Oggins. Business transacted he left the offices.

'Well what's odd about all that?' I asked after he had told me about his experience.

'As I passed the 'Bible' back to Oggins,' Lionel explained,

'I noticed that he had given me his little black Ready Reckoner book instead of the Bible. I am wondering if an affidavit sworn on a Ready Reckoner is as legal as an affidavit sworn on the Bible!'

Swindle, Serenity And Gloom

Josiah James Swindle started the business in 1887 and his successors still run the firm today. He passed it on to his son, Albert, who had a daughter, Charity. In time she married Percy Serenity and their family have continued in the same profession. Since Josiah began to trade the little forest town of Humbury has grown and so the business has expanded. The Serenity family decided they needed a partner to help them run their firm and so Edward joined them. Edward is a true gentleman, kindly to the clients, sympathetic and totally professional. Everyone who encountered Edward agreed that the Serenity family could not have chosen a finer partner.

J. J. Swindle is the only funeral director in Humbury. I always think that Swindle really isn't a very good name for such a firm but that has been the company name for well over a hundred years so why should they change? I phoned Mr Serenity; who surely has the perfect name; and had to tell him that my mother had died.

'You come in and see us,' he said in his gentle manner. 'Edward will take care of everything for you. Don't worry.'

Edward could not have been kinder. Thirty years younger than me but with a wealth of experience he gently steered me through all that had to be done. He phoned the crematorium. 'Hello, Gloom here…' I couldn't believe it! His surname was Gloom! How had J. J. Swindle found this man with such a perfect but curious name?

Swindle, Serenity and Gloom!

The names seemed to have sprung from a morbid nineteenth century novel. If Charles Dickens had created a firm of funeral directors he would surely have chosen names like these.

The day of my mother's funeral came. We assembled in the little church at Whytteford and the sun shone beautifully. As my family processed in, the coffin was placed in front of the altar. It was small as my mother had always been very short and in later years she seemed even smaller. The church windows were open and the musical sounds of the country flooded in and became part of the service. I looked out at the sun shining brightly, bringing warmth and ripeness to autumn fruits. Tears began to flow silently. My mother would have enjoyed such a lovely day.

Afterwards a friend of my parents, who I knew well, came to me and said, 'Your mother may have been over ninety but I still had to watch what I said to her. She always had a witty reply!' This was a small comment but so kind and so true.

The next autumn we reassembled in the same church to bid my father farewell. Edward Gloom had arranged everything to perfection and his gentle, kindly expertise had steered me through a difficult time. My father had loved his garden and so I had made a seasonal wreath to rest on the coffin. Bronzed bracken, hawthorn, nerines and glowing autumn leaves created a fitting tribute. One of the bearers quietly said, 'You could have paid £50 for that and it wouldn't have been as good.'

The little Saxon Church

The coffin was in the hearse. Edward walked down the hill to the church, top hat in hand, leading the way and we again processed into the ancient church. People my parents had known well came to me after the service and said many kind words. These were deeply touching and reassuring; despite their great age my father and mother would be missed in the village. As we left after the service I looked back at the little Saxon church knowing that I would never see it again.

The house had to be cleared. In his final year my father had busily organised many things as if preparing the way for his departure. Documents, photographs and family history had been collected into strong manila envelopes. My parents had lived in their home for nearly fifty years and so there was still much to clear. Long forgotten treasures were rediscovered and consequent reminiscences slowed down the work. Eventually the house was empty. I locked the door, had a final wander round the beautiful garden and lakes my father had created and then climbed into my car and drove away.

I have never returned. I don't want to look back or to go back. Nothing stays the same and returning can be so disappointing and upsetting. The population changes, favourite trees are felled, new homes are built, country lanes are widened and memories become muddled. Time passes and few things stay unaltered.

As I left I knew it was the right time for me to say goodbye to the village that had been part of my family's history for over a century and that I had known for so long. In the churchyard are the graves of my ancestors and so the connection continues, although before long there will be nobody to remember who they were. But no doubt J. J. Swindle, Funeral Directors of Humbury, will still be visiting the little Saxon church tucked away in that corner of The Forest.